GIRL V THE WORLD

Waiting For It

hardie grant EGMONT

Waiting For It
published in 2012 by
Hardie Grant Egmont
Ground Floor, Building 1, 658 Church Street
Richmond, Victoria 3121, Australia
www.hardiegrantegmont.com.au

A CiP record for this title is available from the National Library of Australia

Design by Michelle Mackintosh
Text design and typesetting by Ektavo

Printed in Australia by Griffin Press, an Accredited ISO AS/NZS
14001:2004 Environmental Management System printer.

1 3 5 7 9 10 8 6 4 2

The paper this book is printed on is certified against the
Forest Stewardship Council® Standards. Griffin Press holds
FSC chain of custody certification SGS-COC-005088. FSC
promotes environmentally responsible, socially beneficial
and economically viable management of the world's forests.

Waiting For It

Chrissie Keighery

hardie grant EGMONT

One

Alice Carter was the most popular girl at our primary school, so it's weird knowing she hasn't even squeezed into the top twenty now that we're at high school. She's number twenty-three.

We know this because the boys made a 'hot list' for our year level. It was stuck up next to the timetables on the school events noticeboard. Even though it was taken down quickly – I think it only lasted three hours – pretty much everyone can remember the order.

I pretended not to notice that I was number seventeen.

There were forty girls on the list, so I was in the top half, but still … I felt a long way down.

At least I was put above Alice on the list. I mean, that surprised me at first. But I've learnt the rules are different in high school.

I know lists like that are stupid, of course. And cruel, particularly if you happen to rank very low. But the thing is, stupid or cruel or whatever, I don't reckon there was a single girl in our year who could help looking at that list. The worst thing would be not to have made it onto the list at all. That would be like you didn't even exist!

I can see Alice now as I walk across the quadrangle. She's hugging her books to her chest and looks like she's confused about *everything,* and that doesn't just mean what class she's got next, or where on earth it actually is.

'Hazel!' Alice turns and looks at me as though I'm a lifesaver. 'Do you mind walking with me to maths? I don't know where D12 is.'

Her eyes are darting around as though she thinks I might say no. Which I wouldn't, of course, but it makes her seem unconfident. Plus, her school dress is so long it meets up with her socks with no gap in between.

'Sure,' I say. D12 is one of those portable classrooms the school brought in a couple of weeks ago and plonked at the side of the oval. 'I just have to grab some books from my locker. Wanna come?'

'That would be awesome. Thanks, Hazel!'

I wish for her sake that she'd calm down a bit, but it doesn't seem likely. Alice is kind of bouncy, and always has been. It's one of the things that everyone loved about her in primary school. She pretty much had no vacancies for friends then. People hung around her all the time, and I never really got a chance to get close to her.

But these days, Alice drifts from group to group, like she doesn't quite belong anywhere.

Somehow I've landed on my feet. Not firmly, solidly, on my feet. More like a wobbly, *Oh my god, how is it that I'm in the popular group?* sort of landing. A *will I be able to keep this up?* sort of landing.

But it's way better than not landing at all. There were a couple of spooky months there while I went from group to group at lunchtime, trying to find somewhere to fit.

'It's so hard remembering where everything is, don't you think?' Alice says, interrupting my thoughts as we walk down the breezeway towards the lockers.

She doesn't wait for a response. 'It's like, you just get used to maths being in B block and then they change it and you're supposed to find somewhere else completely. And I really struggled with the homework Mr Cartwright set. Did you get the answer to that last question?'

'Scusi.' Ella Ingram pushes past me to get to her locker. She gets her books and turns around. Ella was number four on the hot list. I guess I can see why, but her face is pretty ordinary. Nothing really stands out there. Her hair isn't that different to mine. It's sort of mid-length and browny blonde and she wears it in a ponytail with blue clips at the sides. But I don't think the reason she made number four has anything to do with her face or her hair. Her school jumper is tucked up twice, like mine is. But it's way tighter, like mine would be if Mum had let me get the size I wanted. And her skirt only comes halfway down her thighs. You can see that Ella's got proper boobs, a proper waist and really long legs.

I haven't bothered asking Mum to take up my skirt. She'd probably say no, and even if she said yes, she'd never get around to it. She's too busy now that she's got a stupid boyfriend.

'So?' Alice prompts me. 'The last question?'

I watch as Ella heads off with her books.

'We have until the end of the week, Alice,' I say, turning to her. 'I haven't started it yet.'

Alice looks surprised. To be honest, I *have* done the homework sheet, except for the tricky last question, but there are people all around us and I don't want them to think I'm super keen or anything.

I get my books. Alice stands beside me, quietly now. She's about a head taller than me, but she's skinnier. Her school jumper is baggy and not tucked up at all, and you can tell that she's completely, totally flat. When I look down at my own chest, I'm not exactly thrilled with what I see. Or don't see. But at least there are two little bumps that show some promise for the future.

I wonder if the boys noticed that, even as I remind myself that the hot list is stupid and cruel.

'Hannah helped me, you know.' Alice is talking more quietly now, like she finally gets that I might not want everyone to hear us. 'So if you need help …'

Alice keeps talking, but I drift off, thinking about the list again. Hannah didn't even make the list. There are forty-four girls in our year, so four haven't made the list at all, including Hannah. She went to the same primary school as Alice and me. She's kind of fat, but it's not just fat under her school polo. It's as if she 'developed' too quickly, and she's trying to hide it. In primary school, 'developing' was embarrassing. Hannah was the first girl, by ages, to get her period. Everyone knew, because she would only go into the one toilet cubicle that had a sanitary dispenser thing.

I would have hated to get my period way before anyone else, but it's really stressing me out that I still haven't got it now. I'm thirteen and four months, and … nothing's happening.

I sneak a sideways glance at Alice as she chats away. I wonder if she has hers yet.

Olympia skids across the floor between me and Alice. Her hand is on her locker door, but her eyes dart up the hallway to where Edi is.

'Hi, Hazel,' she says, ignoring Alice.

She grabs her maths book and slams the locker door as though she's in a hurry. But we've got plenty of time to get to maths.

'I'm walking with Edi,' she calls over her shoulder as she dashes ahead. 'You and Alice can talk maths together.'

I smile. On the outside. But inside it feels like a little stab. Olympia is part of my group, but she says stuff like this to me all the time. Cutting stuff. She must've heard Alice going on about homework. I would've liked to walk with her and Edi – they're in my group, after all.

That's the thing with Olympia. I'm not even sure if she was trying to be mean or if it just came out that way. Sometimes she's really nice to me. One thing I *am* sure about is that Olympia takes every opportunity to get Edi to herself. But I guess Jess and I are a bit like that too.

Edi is number one on the hot list, and she's number one in our group, too. That's just how it is.

'You go ahead if you like, Hazel,' Alice says.

For a second, I think about leaving Alice behind and

catching up to Edi and Olympia. But I can't. It would look too try-hard, for one. And secondly, it would be mean to Alice.

Even from the back, you can see why Edi is number one on the list. I would have put her there as well. Her mum is Indian, and Edi has long dark hair that she straightens even though she doesn't really need to. It really gleams, and her eyes do too. Even the braces on her teeth look good, like a little bit of extra jewellery you can't get told off for wearing. Plus, she's incredibly cool. I was with Edi when we saw the hot list for the first time. She rolled those eyes like it was no big deal. That's how cool she is.

Alice and I are just about to walk up the portable stairs when Nicholas Bradbury flies down them. I think he's definitely going to knock us over, but he just manages to stop in time.

'Morning, Hazel! Morning, Alice!' he says, his whole face screwing up with his grin.

'Morning, Nick,' we say together.

I don't know how he does it, maybe it's his Down syndrome, but Nick stretches his grin even wider and launches into the song we've been learning for music performance. He sings loud and strong and over-the-top, using his fist as a microphone like he's on stage.

His free arm waves about so much that Alice and I have to lean back.

'I'm going to do that homework tonight,' I whisper to Alice as Nick sings. 'If I get stuck, I'll message you, yeah?'

There's a smile between us that makes me glad I've said it. It's a *how weird is life? Can you believe how much has changed?* exchange, and Nick has caused it somehow.

I can tell Alice loves Nick as much as I do. I think it's the fact that he doesn't worry about all the stuff everyone else worries about. He's just really *honest,* I guess.

Alice gives me a little nod as the three of us break into the chorus, Nick's voice ringing out over the top of ours. Laughing, Alice and I head up the stairs, waving goodbye to Nick, who sees some other students and backtracks.

In D12, Edi, Jess and Olympia are sitting at a hexagonal table at the back of the room. They are leaning towards each other, plotting something. When she sees me, Jess jumps up and almost runs over.

'Saved you a seat, Haze,' she says breathlessly, threading her arm through mine.

'Cool,' I reply, though Jess saving me a seat is nothing out of the ordinary. What is strange, though, is her expression. She looks pleased with herself when she smiles. Something's behind the smile. I know there's news. It's almost bursting out of her.

I feel Alice peel off me. I can see her scanning her options before she takes a seat next to Erin and Briana at the front. It's not like anything gets said, like there are any spoken rules about who sits where, but I know if Alice sat at our table, the others would think it was wrong.

Alice hasn't got how to fold her jumper up the right way, and she doesn't know not to act too keen about homework, but she's got this right.

'Oh my god,' Jess says, as she practically pushes me into my seat. She leans forward. Edi and Olympia do the same, so I copy.

'All right,' Edi says, 'whatever you've got happening tonight, cancel it. Caravan meeting, five o'clock.'

Olympia nods as she sits back in her chair. 'Yeah, I'm

skipping basketball. This is more important.'

'Why? What's up?' I ask.

I love our caravan meetings, but they're normally on Friday so we can go through everything that's happened during the week. Something extra important is obviously going on for a Tuesday meeting, and it seems that I'm the only one who doesn't know what it is.

Mr Cartwright walks in.

'I'll tell you tonight,' Jess whispers, as Nick closes the door behind Mr Cartwright like he's royalty.

Mr C is pretty strict. You're not allowed to talk to each other during class unless it's about work, but Jess squeezes in a few more words before he begins the lesson.

'Do I look any different?' she asks, posing for me by flicking her ponytail and jutting out a shoulder.

I don't quite know what to say. Jess doesn't look any different to me, but that's obviously not what she wants to hear. I do a quick scan, checking her hair, face, clothes. Nup, no signs of difference.

Luckily it's too risky to reply anyway. Mr C can really crack it and I hate being told off.

Suddenly I get it. It's like a weight that lands in my chest and sinks down into my tummy.

I'm pretty sure I know what the meeting's going to be about.

As I walk home from school, I'm getting kind of excited about the caravan meeting. I mean, if it's about what I think it's going to be about, it'll be hard in some ways. But I'm dying to know what Jess has to say. I want to know as much as possible before it happens to me – if it ever does. Jess is the perfect person to get information from. Even though she goes way, way off track at times, she also doesn't hold anything back. With Jess, I'll get all the juicy details.

I organise a to-do list in my head so I'll make it to the caravan meeting on time.

1. Tell Mum that I'm not going to be able to cook the raspberry and white chocolate muffins we'd been planning to make this arvo.

We do stuff like that most Tuesday afternoons when Romy's at netball practice and not around to guts them all down before they even cool. I feel a bit bad about it, but I'm pretty sure Mum will be okay. We can always make them tomorrow.

2. Get my clean clothes out of the laundry.

Luckily, I put practically my whole wardrobe in there last night and since Mum has Tuesdays off work and she always does stuff around the house, they'll be ready. I choose an outfit in my head to save time. Black jeans and my purple T-shirt. Oh, and my black Cons. Edi loves them.

3. Have some afternoon tea and a drink.

Then I'll be ready to go.

I get home in record time and groan as soon as I see the Feral's rusty bike on our front porch. Just the sight of it makes me want to vomit or something. It's messy and it's right beside the door and it's not even locked up, though you'd have to be pretty desperate to want to steal it. My big sister Romy made up his nickname. It so suits him.

I stay on the porch for a moment, even though it's taking away some of the time I've saved with my to-do list. I can't believe he's here. Like, even though I'm not going to be able to hang out with Mum today, *she* didn't know that. It's really rude.

I brace myself as I open the front door. Straight away, the stink of his loser-scented candles gets me. He's standing in the hallway like he owns the house or something.

'Hi, buddy,' he says, even though he's not my buddy. 'How was school?'

He's barefoot and his trackie dacks have paint splatters all over them and the crotch is halfway down his legs. Not in a cool way. His hair is in dreadlocks that hang down his back. If you didn't know he showers for long enough to use up all our hot water, you'd think he was dirty.

'Fine,' I say shortly. 'Where's Mum?'

'Hi, Hazel,' Mum says, poking her head out of the kitchen. 'I got all the stuff for muffins. Jason's made them before. He's going to help.'

'Really?' I say, and now I don't feel bad about going out one little bit. Like I'd really want to hang out with Mum and *him*. 'Actually, I have to go to Edi's.'

'Oh … okay,' Mum says. 'That's a shame.'

'Yeah, *totally*,' I reply and I hope she gets the sarcastic tone but she just starts talking to *him* about some stupid yoga class so I don't even bother saying anything else. I just drop my schoolbag and go into the laundry.

'Oh my god,' I yell out. The laundry basket is still full of my dirty clothes. Mum comes to the laundry door.

'Mum, *all* my clothes are in here,' I moan. 'You didn't wash them!' I pick up my black jeans. They're sodden with water from a towel. In fact, nothing in the basket is even wearable.

Mum leans against the door like it's no big deal.

'I didn't do any chores today, Hazel,' she says dreamily and she's not even *apologising*. 'It was such a nice day. Jason took me for a picnic.'

I shake my head and walk past her to my room. Honestly, I don't even think she notices the smoke coming out of my ears.

I think about borrowing something from Romy, but if I do that without her permission she'll kill me. I have to settle for a stupid T-shirt that I've had since I was about *ten*. It's got a daisy with eyes and a mouth on the front. I throw on some old jeans that are hand-me-downs from Romy. They're supposed to be skinny legs but they're huge on me. Way cool.

I don't even have any afternoon tea. They're in the kitchen. *Together.*

I slam the front door as I go.

I'm calmer by the time I get to Edi's.

Edi's house is amazing. It looks like a ship, all sharp angles and loads of windows everywhere. But we hardly ever go into the actual house. I walk down the driveway. The caravan is off to the left at the bottom of the garden, overlooking the sparkling in-ground pool.

Edi told me that the caravan has only been out of the backyard once. They drove it up the coast on a family holiday. Edi reckons they only lasted a few days before they drove each other mad and came back home. Now it's her own private space.

Edi is at the doorway. She waves and comes out to get me. Jess and Olympia follow her out. Even though I'm on time, they're all there and I get a funny feeling, like they might have arranged to arrive earlier. It doesn't help that all of them look really cool and I'm standing here in this random outfit. I wonder if I should tell them about what just happened at home. About Mum not doing the washing, and the Feral hanging around. But I decide against it. They'd probably think Mum's not being a proper mum and even though that's pretty much how I'm feeling at the moment, I don't really want them to know. The whole thing is just embarrassing.

'Haze,' Edi says, giving me a hug. 'I'm glad you're finally here.'

Jess gives me a big squeeze, even though I saw everyone just a couple of hours ago.

'We've been waiting for you,' Olympia says, and she hugs me too. It's a quick one, but it's still a hug.

It's nice to know that they've waited for me to get into the juicy details, even if Jess has obviously told them both *something*. The funny feeling shrinks until it's only a tiny speck of worry inside me.

'It took me a while to get my outfit right,' I say, running my hands down my baggy jeans. 'You like it?'

They all giggle.

'It's gorgeous!' Jess says.

'Cool daisy ... love the face,' Edi adds.

'Idiot,' Olympia says, but she's grinning at me.

I love making the girls laugh. That's kind of how I ended up in the group. There was an interschool tennis match. I was a bit nervous when I found out who was on my team. Playing tennis with the coolest girls in our whole year? Great. I'm a hit, trip and giggle sort of tennis player.

But the girls thought I was really funny. Especially when I tripped over my laces, fell into the net and brought it down. It was a total accident, but I played it up after that.

Anyway, it worked. At school on Monday, Edi beckoned me over. The number one girl on the hot list called *me* over.

I glance around the caravan as we head inside. Even though I've been here quite a few times I'm still impressed. Edi has decorated the van really well. The curtains are drawn. They are a deep maroon, and so is the quilt cover on the bed in the corner. There are about a million cushions in maroon, white and pink piled up on the bed. When Edi closes the door behind us, it's like we're in a beautiful cocoon.

'So. Can I start?' Jess asks, looking at each of us with wide eyes.

'Let's get comfy first,' Edi says.

She slides across the lime green bench seat at the little table. Olympia quickly slides in next to her, like she's racing me for the next-to-Edi position. Which is pretty dumb because I wouldn't do that anyway. It wouldn't be worth getting Olympia mad.

I sit on the other side. Jess stands, waiting for us to settle. I think back to a few months ago, when it was Olympia's turn to make the announcement. It wasn't a surprise. But Jess? She's always been like me, development wise. I guess that's changed.

'Okay, Jess. Spill!' Olympia says, looking satisfied now she's next to Edi.

'As in, spill the *relevant* bits,' Edi adds, laughing.

Jess loves to tell a story. But she goes into so much detail that the simplest story in the world turns into a very long soap opera.

'Well,' Jess says, taking a deep breath, 'last night, about five-thirty, I was walking Frodo. He likes to go to the doggy park where you can let the dogs off their leashes so they can smell each other's butts. Which is totally gross but it's just their way of – '

'Jess!' we all say together.

Jess grins. 'Okay. Right. So, anyway, I felt something weird. Like something was seeping into my undies, but I wasn't sure. I had to wait until Frodo did his poo. But finally I got back home and I went to the loo. Hey, I rhymed! Poo and loo.'

Olympia taps the table.

'There *was* something in my undies, but I still wasn't sure because it was browny-red, not reddy-red, and it was only a little bit.'

'That's normal,' Edi says. She's been getting her period for ages. Since way before I joined the group.

'Yeah, that's what Mum said,' Jess says. 'You know, Mum predicted that I'd get it really soon. Because of my boobs getting bigger and stuff.'

Jess cups her hands under her boobs, pushing them up and together, and waggles her head. We're all laughing.

Inside, though, I wonder what Jess means by *and stuff*. Her boobs are about the same size as mine. *Maybe she means something else ... like pubic hair?* I know it's stupid, but I wonder if maybe there's a particular number of hairs you grow, say twenty-two, then *whoosh*, you get your period. But Jess doesn't say anything about that, she just keeps talking about her mum's reaction.

'Honestly, even though Mum's been predicting it, she was more emotional than me! She was all, *Oh, my little Jessie! Your entrance into womanhood!* Blah blah. She even teared up!'

'That's so cute,' Olympia says.

'Yeah, I can so imagine her saying that,' Edi adds. 'I love your mum.'

It's a bit awkward for me, since I haven't even met Jess's mum. I just nod, but it makes me think about my mum. She's been predicting that I'll get my period for *ages*. You'd think she'd be worried about me. You'd think she would want to take me to the doctor's to get checked out. She said she'd make an appointment, but she hasn't.

Probably because she's too busy being all lovey-dovey with the Feral.

'Mum *was* cute,' Jess agrees. 'I already had some pads that she bought for me. You just peel the sticky bit off the back and they sort of tape into your undies,' she explains, turning to me.

It's like she's suddenly the expert, as if she's reminding everyone that I'm the only one who doesn't have her period yet. Maybe I'm being sensitive, but it's annoying.

'Then Mum took me out for pizza,' continues Jess. 'Just the two of us, to celebrate. Luke spat it because he wanted pizza too, but he had to have leftover spag bol, which was actually from two days before and he reckoned it probably had salmonella or something. But on the way to the pizza place it was, like, *gross*. I could feel the blood dripping out of me and I had my skinny jeans on and I kept wondering if anyone walking past could see there was a big lump in my undies!'

That makes me feel a bit sick. It's more gory than juicy. But I still wish it was me telling the story. I'm officially the last one in our group to get it, and I'm older than all of them. You'd think we'd get it in order of age.

Then it hits me. We aren't getting it in order of age, but we are getting it in order. In the order as we appear on the hot list! Edi is number one. Olympia is number eight and Jess is number ten. And I'm number seventeen. Unlucky last!

It could just be coincidence … but maybe it's not? Maybe the two things are connected somehow?

'You've got to try tampons,' Edi says. 'They're so much better.'

'Yeah,' Olympia agrees. 'I've been practising and I'm totally going to use tampons next time.'

'It's not hard once you get the angle right,' Edi explains. 'And you can't feel tampons at all. Plus, pads can get smelly when they're soaked.'

Now I feel really queasy and the queasiness is mixed

up with frustration. Not only am I the only one who isn't developing properly, but Edi has graduated to tampons and Olympia won't be far behind.

Edi grabs four cans of Coke from the titchy kitchen cupboard and we crack them open.

'To Jess,' Edi says, holding up her can to be clinked.

'Who is now a woman!' Olympia adds.

Jess bows and does a quick Michael Jackson moonwalk. We all clink cans.

I take a sip, keeping a smile stuck to my face. It doesn't seem to trick anyone.

'You're next, Haze. Any day now,' Olympia says, and she says it kindly.

I'm used to her being the most tricky one in the group. She seems to go hot and cold on me all the time, and I reckon it's mostly to do with her wanting to be the closest to Edi, but it still hurts sometimes. Now she's being super nice and it makes me feel wobbly. Everyone's looking at me.

'Yeah, hopefully it'll turn up before we finish high school,' I say. 'Or maybe I'll be walking around when I'm about forty-five and I have long saggy boobs down to my ankles and I'll be saying, *any day now.*'

It's supposed to be a joke, but it doesn't come out like that. Not really.

'You know, it's horrible sometimes,' Edi says. 'I get cramps and they really hurt.'

'I get seriously bloated,' Olympia adds. 'It's disgusting.'

'Yeah, don't rush it,' Edi adds. 'Once you get it, you've got it until you're like ... *old.* Think about it. Once every six weeks, for four days. For the rest of your life.'

'You're lucky,' Olympia says. 'I get mine every four weeks and it lasts for five days at least. It's like, wrong!'

Edi and Olympia are joining forces to make me feel better. It's working. I might be the last girl on earth to get my period, but I love these chats. I've never had friends who talk like this. It's so *open,* and it makes me think that maybe Olympia does like me, deep down. Maybe she's just a bit cold with everyone.

I look over at Jess. I don't think she's really noticed how the others are trying to make me feel better. She's just standing there with her nose screwed up, hands on hips.

'Every *four weeks?*' she repeats, as though it's just dawned on her that this might not be so much fun after a while. 'No way I'm doing it that often!'

'Not *you*, of course, Jess,' I say and the giggles get me. I snort a bit of foamy Coke out of my nose. It sets everyone off and I do it again, kind of on purpose to keep the laughs going, and because I don't want to be a downer or anything.

'We've got swimming tomorrow,' Edi suddenly says after the laughing dies down. 'Will you tell Mr J that you've got it?'

'Nup. I'm going to get a note from Mum and go to the library,' Jess replies. 'No way am I going to be like Lola!'

Jess draws up her upper lip so her teeth look big, like Lola's. 'Guess why I can't go *swimming* today?' She sounds just like Lola, except Lola didn't actually say that. She just sat at the side of the pool instead of going inside and doing something else, which totally made it *obvious*.

'The boys would all have known,' Olympia says, rolling her eyes.

The conversation switches to boys. Edi has a crush on Archie, a really hot boy from the year above us. It's a fun conversation and it's even more fun when Edi stands in a corner with her back to us and makes it look like someone is kissing her.

'Archie, Archie,' she says as her hands wander over her back. Then she flops back onto the bed with a sigh, grabbing a cushion from the bed. She gives the cushion a long kiss, laughing as she does it.

I can't see what her lips are doing because they're stuffed into the cushion, but I know that Edi's had real-life kissing practice. She was going with Oscar Poulson for more than a month at the beginning of the year. It was before we became friends, but I saw her hooking up with him at a blue-light disco. They used tongues and everything.

The closest I've come is when Tyson Banks came up to me in the playground in year five, kissed my cheek and ran away. It wasn't a real kiss and there were definitely no tongues. I've *imagined* kissing someone, though. Then again, I've imagined getting my period too. It doesn't really count, I guess.

Edi is still cushion-kissing when my phone beeps. There's a new text from Mum.

Just got called into work. Maybe you and Romy can help Jason with dinner? Xx

I groan. Surely Mum wouldn't leave the Feral alone in our house. Would she?

Three

I'm coming around the corner when I see Romy up ahead, just outside our house. She sees me and waits out the front until I catch up.

'Mum's left the Feral alone in there,' Romy whispers, pointing at our front door.

I nod and roll my eyes. Romy moves the Feral's bike to the end of the porch and tucks the handlebars under the railing so you can't see it from the street. Don't know why. It would serve him right if it got stolen.

'Unbelievable,' I say.

I'm so glad that Romy is here. That at least *she* understands, even if Mum has gone mental.

'I wonder if he can cook?' she says, fishing around for her keys. 'I hope so. I'm starving but can't be stuffed cooking.'

Romy loves food, but she's straying from the point.

'It's *irresponsible*,' I say, to bring her back to it.

Romy shrugs. 'I guess it means she trusts him,' she says.

'I guess that means she's gone mad,' I say.

Romy smiles at me over her shoulder, like I've made a joke. Which I haven't. I'm about to tell her that I'm completely serious but she's already opening the door.

He's standing in the hallway again.

'Hey, guys,' he says. 'How was netball, Romy? Did you have fun with your friends, Hazel?'

'It was okay,' I say.

'We won,' says Romy.

He's leaning against the wall in our hallway so we have to walk under the arch of his arm. It's really annoying. It's even more annoying that when we get past him, he charges back in front to lead the way down the hall.

'Dee Dee got called into work,' he says as if we didn't already know that about our own mother. He heads into the kitchen. I'm annoyed when my tummy rumbles. It smells good. 'Someone was sick. It's just for a few hours.'

Mum's name is Diana. Romy and I get to call her Dee sometimes, because that's how her name came out when Romy was little.

No-one calls her Dee Dee. I narrow my eyes and shoot a look at Romy. She rolls her eyes back at me, but there's a twist at the corner of her mouth that's confusing. It looks like a mini-smile.

I don't think it's funny. At all.

'I've made a chicken curry,' he says, opening the lid of a saucepan to show us. Romy practically sticks her head in the pot, breathing in the aroma.

He walks over to the bench. 'Oh, and some raspberry and white chocolate muffins. Here, try some.'

He's made *my* muffins!

He cuts a muffin in half and slathers the pieces with soft butter that he's left in the pantry instead of in the fridge where it should be. I wouldn't even normally have butter on this kind of muffin, but I know Romy would. She'd put butter on anything.

He hands one half of the muffin to me and one to Romy, as though we've agreed to try it, which we haven't. He doesn't even use plates. He just stands there and waits for us to take a bite.

I put my piece back on the bench, willing Romy to do the same. I'm thinking it could be like a protest. Well, it could be, except that Romy takes a bite. Then another.

'Yum,' she says, with her mouth full.

I can tell by the way she says it that the muffin is really good. It looks really fluffy compared to ones I've made before with Mum and it makes me even more hungry.

The Feral grins at her.

'Not hungry, Hazel?' he asks, turning to me.

I shake my head firmly, willing my tummy not to rumble. I don't feel like eating the muffins *I* was supposed to make with Mum and I don't feel like answering him. Romy's already finished her half, and I can tell she's not looking at me on purpose.

Our home phone rings. The phone is at the end of the

kitchen bench, close to the Feral. I reach over to grab it, just in case he thinks he's going to answer it.

It's Mum. *Dee Dee.*

'Hi, hon,' she says. 'Just wanted to check that you're all home. Is Romy there too? And Jason?'

'Romy's here,' I reply. 'And Jason was here when we got home. By himself, *actually.*'

I say the last bit as I take the phone out of the kitchen and down the hall. I don't think he heard me, but I don't really care if he did.

'Okay, okay. Good.' Mum's voice falters like it does when she's feeling guilty. Which she should. It's really awkward for Romy and me to come home and have him there.

'So, has Jason made his chicken curry? I hope so.' Mum says it as though she's had it before. Probably when Romy and I were at Dad and Lisa's, I suppose. When we were out of the way.

I don't say anything.

'Hazel? Are you okay? Is everything all right?'

'Yep,' I say, too quickly for it to be true.

Everything is not all right. I need to talk to her. I need to tell her about everyone else getting their periods and get her to make a doctor's appointment to find out what's wrong with me.

I can't believe she's let all this happen. Mum met the Feral at yoga and the next thing you know, they're an item and he's practically *living* at our house. I've already told her she's rushing into it. Mum actually laughed when I said that. Then she made some sarcastic comment about how she and Dad have been divorced for six years and she hadn't even had a date since then, until she met Jason. The whole thing was leading up to her telling me that Dad didn't waste any time getting into a relationship with Lisa.

I hate it when Mum says stuff like that. It's not like we don't all know that Dad got with Lisa really quickly after they split, but there's no point talking about it all the time. Lisa is a bit uptight, but she's basically *normal.* Not like the Feral. And Romy and I just go there Wednesdays and every second weekend, and sometimes less than that, because they're always going overseas on business trips. So it's not like Lisa is invading our actual *home.*

'So,' Mum says into the silence, 'I'll see you guys in about half an hour, okay?'

'Okay,' I say. I walk into the lounge room and hang up.

The Feral has pushed our coffee table to one side of the room and left his yoga mat just sitting there in the middle of the living room. I give the corner of it a little flick with my foot. The way he leaves his stuff all over the place makes our house feel less *ours*.

When I go into my room, I see the photo of me, Dad and Romy the time he took us to Luna Park.

Dad's the opposite of the Feral, really neat and clean-shaven with short hair. Definitely no dreadlocks. I wonder for the millionth time how Mum could go from Dad to *that*.

I'm still in my bedroom when I hear Mum come home a bit later. The door is closed but I can hear voices coming from the kitchen. It's Mum, Romy and the Feral.

I pick up the photo of Dad and go back to the lounge room. A short burst of laughter streams down the hallway from the kitchen. It's really annoying to hear that one of the laughs is Romy's.

I put the photo on the mantelpiece. There are already

loads of photos up there of me and Romy and Mum, but there aren't any of Dad. I tuck the photo in among them so it doesn't stand out. It feels better that he's up there.

Now Dad can keep an eye on the Feral.

'Can you set the good table, please, Hazel,' Mum says
when she forces me to come out of my room again.

'Why?' I ask.

'Because we have a guest,' she says.

I look away and roll my eyes so she can't see. For one
thing, our *guest* seems to be at our place a little bit too
much to be called that. I mean, he *made* the dinner. And
for another thing, it seems pretty ridiculous to set the good
table when he's flopping about with his old trackie dacks
and bare feet.

The good table is in the lounge room. We each take a bowl of chicken curry in there. Nobody notices Dad up on the mantelpiece, which is good. Mum would probably chuck it if she did. Plus, it's kind of cool knowing he's there when no-one else does.

'Oh. My. God,' Romy says. 'This chicken curry is amazing. What's in it?' I give her a kick under the table as I take a mouthful. It is pretty good, but I wish Romy wouldn't be so over-the-top about it.

'Why, thank you, Romy,' the Feral says. 'It's an old family recipe, but I think what makes it special is focusing on good energy while you cook it. A pinch of care, a dash of tenderness, you know?'

I look up at Dad. I swear he's gone pale.

'Sweet,' Romy says, as though what he's just said are not the words of a madman. It's seriously annoying.

'So, what's happening with you, Hazel?' Mum asks and I know she's just trying to get me to talk because I've barely said a word. She's probably worried that I'm making our *guest* uncomfortable.

'Nothing much,' I say. *Except that I'm number seventeen*

on the hot list. Except that everyone else has got their period and there's probably something really wrong with me and I'll probably end up dropping off the list altogether and be a little girl forever. Except that your boyfriend is taking over our lives.

'Dee Dee tells me you've got some really nice friends, Hazel,' the Feral says. 'That's great. True friends are good for your chakras. The input of energy …'

'I have homework,' I say. I can't listen to any more of this stuff. Mum glares at me. 'May I be excused?' I add.

Mum and the Feral exchange looks like *I'm* the problem.

'Okay,' Mum says.

As I go to my room, I hear Romy's voice. 'Can I have seconds, please?'

I close my bedroom door so I don't have to hear them all talking.

V

After dinner, the Feral goes back to his place to finish a painting or something, thank god, so I finally have Mum and Romy to myself.

'So,' I say, while we're doing the giant load of dishes the Feral's just left there on the bench. Mum's washing and Romy and I are drying. 'Jess got her period.'

I pause, waiting for Mum and Romy to react to the news. But it seems I have to spell it out.

'I'm the last one in my group to get it now. I might be the last girl in my year, even.'

'Or the last girl in the universe,' Romy teases, flicking me with her tea towel.

'This is serious,' I say, and just to prove it, I don't even flick her back. 'Mum, you *have* to take me to the doctor. We need to find out what's wrong with me!'

Mum doesn't reply straight away. She carefully washes the last plate before she turns to me.

'Hazel, I know you're worried, but everyone's different. Like Jason says, we all have to learn to be happy in our own skin and it's really negative to work against yourself. You don't need to see a doctor, Haze. Your beautiful body will be true to its own timing.'

Now I can see why it's taken her so long to answer. She had to channel the Feral. It's like he's taken over her brain!

I'm furious and I'm hurt and I wish he would disappear from our lives and from Mum's brain so she could go back to being a proper mum who cares about me and would definitely take me to the doctor.

I throw my tea towel on the dish rack and storm out of the kitchen. If there was a door into the hallway, I would slam it. I storm down towards my room.

My bedroom has a slammable door, so even though Mum totally hates it when we do it, I give the door a good, satisfying slam.

I lean my head against the door. I can hear Romy trying to talk Mum into taking me to the doctor, and that makes me feel a bit better about her being all nice to the Feral at dinnertime. And then I hear them still talking about me but I can't hear what they're saying.

I flop onto my bed and pull the covers over my head to shut out the world.

Five minutes later, Mum knocks on my door. 'Hazel?' she says.

I keep my head under the covers and don't answer her. She goes away.

A bit later, I hear someone come in. I peer out from under the covers and see Romy as she sits on my bed.

'Haze, I'll take you to the doctor's if you want,' she says.

I push the covers away and sit up.

'Thanks,' I say. 'But don't you think it should be Mum who takes me? You know, this is all because of the Feral. He's ruining everything. I just wish things were back to normal.'

Romy lies down next to me, looking up at the ceiling.

'I don't think we should call him that anymore,' she says. When she's the one who actually made up the name in the first place. 'The thing is, we might get into the habit and then we might end up saying it in front of Mum and that wouldn't be fair to her, you know? We don't want to hurt Mum, do we?'

I shake my head. Of course I don't want to hurt Mum. I just want her back.

'Okay,' I say tiredly.

Romy gives my back a little rub.

'Think about it, Hazel,' she continues. 'He's not that bad. At least he's interested enough to ask us lots of questions, even if they are a bit drippy. And Mum just reckons that you're perfect the way you are. She says you're not sick so there's no need to take you to the doctor.'

I bite my lip so I don't cry. I'm *not* perfect the way I am. That's the problem. There's something wrong with me. Something is stopping me getting my period. Even now it's running around in my head like it did at dinnertime. I could be stuck as a kid forever. I'll slip off the hot list altogether. Then I'll probably be out of the popular group and … It's exhausting just to think about it.

Romy turns on her side to look at me. 'The period stuff aside,' she says, 'I think you have to ask yourself whether it's Jason you don't like – or whether you just don't like Mum having a boyfriend.'

She squeezes my arm, gets up off my bed and walks to the door. She's leaving me with the question, but it's one I don't think I can answer. There are too many thoughts swirling in my head.

Maybe I *am* being unfair about 'Jason'? Maybe it's all this stuff about not getting my period and the hot list and worrying about keeping up with my friends that's making me like this. But I just feel so mad with Mum, and so annoyed at him.

'It's him, of course.' I say it to myself, under the covers, but I'm not so sure it's true anymore. Maybe I'll feel clearer about it when things settle down with Jess. That thought makes me feel a bit better. By the time I get to school tomorrow, Jess will probably be used to having her period. It won't be that big a deal. She probably won't even mention it.

I let that thought drift around in my head and finally fall asleep.

'Can you check the back of my dress, Haze?' Jess whispers.

I sigh. I'm glad that school is just about over. I've checked the back of Jess's dress about a hundred times already today.

So much for things settling down. So much for Jess not mentioning having her period.

I wonder if I could make this into a career? Professional

back-of-dress-checker. I reckon I'd get the top job – I've got good experience.

'Haze?' Jess hassles. 'Did you look?'

'Hang on,' I say. I've had three classes with Jess today, and she's asked this every time she's got up from her seat. Part of me wonders if Jess is just trying to rub in the fact that she has her period and I don't.

I glance at the back of her dress yet again. But then I see it. There is actually a spot there. It's only small, but it's definitely blood.

'Stop walking,' I say.

I say it a bit like there's a big hairy spider on the back of her dress. I feel a bit panicked. This is serious! There are people *everywhere* in the quadrangle, like there always is after the bell goes. Jess would *die* if anyone saw the blood!

It's a warm day and we're not wearing our jumpers, so I can't tell Jess to tie one around her waist. Luckily, Edi and Olympia come up. I point to the spot.

Olympia thinks the most quickly. 'All right,' she says, her voice calm and even, 'Jess, we're going to walk behind you to the toilets. No-one will be able to see.'

We get Jess safely to the toilets. Jess races into one of the cubicles to change her pad.

'We need hairspray,' Edi says.

No-one really questions her. Sometimes when we're on Facebook Edi has to sign out because she has to do housework or washing, so I guess she knows stuff like this.

Olympia nods. 'Lucky you've been getting us to check all day!' she calls to Jess over the toilet door. 'And lucky you spotted it so soon, Hazel,' she says to me.

Jess flushes the toilet and comes out to wash her hands.

'Imagine if one of the boys saw it first!' says Jess, drying her hands on the front of her dress.

I guess I should feel bad to discover that Jess was getting Edi and Olympia to check her dress, as well as me. But it actually makes me feel better. It means Jess wasn't just rubbing it in. She was honestly worried.

Olympia races off to get hairspray out of her locker. When she comes back, her face is flushed. I can tell she's been running and I get a funny feeling. I wonder if she would do the same for me? But here we are, all sticking together. And right now, Olympia feels like a good friend.

At the back of my mind I'm worried that I'll be late meeting Romy at the bus stop. We might miss the first bus to Dad and Lisa's, but this is more important. I can always send Romy a text.

Jess stands there in her dress while Edi sprays the spot with hairspray and sponges it with cold water and paper towel. Then Edi lifts the back of Jess's dress right up to dry it under the hand dryer. Jess's undies are showing, and she keeps trying to turn to see if the spot's gone.

Someone comes into the toilets and we all look up in panic.

It's Alice. Jess quickly pulls her dress down to cover her bum, but the back is still wet.

'Oh,' Alice says, stopping in the doorway. 'Everything all right?' she asks, and I can tell by her voice she's figured out what's happened.

'Yeah, fine,' Jess says. It's probably just because she's embarrassed, but the way Jess speaks to Alice is a bit sharp. I feel bad for Alice because it's like she doesn't know where to look.

'Don't tell anyone, okay?' Edi snaps.

Alice looks hurt. 'I wouldn't do that,' she says and her normally bouncy voice is small.

The saying *see ya, wouldn't wanna be ya* jumps around in my head as Alice turns and walks out of the loos. I wish I had said something nice to her.

We get Jess's dress dry with the hand dryer and then I race off to meet Romy at the bus stop. I can't wait to see Dad. He was overseas last week, so Romy and I didn't get to see him for our usual Wednesday sleepover.

I love their apartment. It's big and shiny and new and you can see the city lights at night.

And I need a break from the whole Mum and Jason thing.

Five

Even the lift at Dad and Lisa's apartment is amazing. It's on the corner of the building and it's made of glass, so you can see the whole world as you go up and down. Romy and I both dive at the button for the fifteenth floor. I'm first, as usual.

'Wonder what's for dinner,' Romy says. 'Sick soup?'

I'm glad I've just had a chocolate bar on the bus so I'm not too hungry. Lisa isn't much of a cook, and Dad's probably never cooked a meal in his life.

'Vegetable vomit?' I join in.

I like this game, but Romy always starts it because she's so obsessed with food. I'm sure it was the chicken curry that made Romy go all soft on the Fer– ... on Jason.

It was pretty good, much as I hate to admit it.

The lift door opens and Dad and Lisa are standing in the doorway of the apartment. Dad opens his arms and I run into them.

'Hey, Dad,' Romy says, avoiding the hug and walking down the hallway.

Romy is sort of a mummy's girl. I'm definitely more of a daddy's girl.

'Hey, munchkin,' Dad says, landing a kiss on the top of my head as he lets me go. He holds me out at arm's length to get a better look at me, then pulls me into a big hug. 'How's my baby girl?'

I should tell Dad sometime to stop saying things like that. Who knows, it might be this kind of stuff that's making it harder for me to grow up properly. But it never feels like the right time to get him to stop. And part of me never wants him to.

When Dad has finished choking me and ruining my

hair, I put my bags down and give Lisa a hug. Out of the corner of my eye, I see Dad taking my bags into the apartment.

He hates mess. So does Lisa. There's no way they'd leave yoga mats in the lounge room or dishes everywhere. They're both wearing their home clothes, their *relaxing* clothes, but even their relaxing clothes are neat and tidy. Lisa is wearing a long jumper and beige leggings, her blonde hair tied back in a tight high ponytail. Dad's wearing tan pants and a polo shirt. His hair is cut even shorter than usual and it makes me think of Jason with his dreadlocks and his paint-splattered trackie dacks.

'I've made an eggplant and asparagus quiche,' Lisa says as we go into the lounge room. Romy and I exchange grimaces when Lisa's not looking. 'We can eat whenever you're ready.'

'I just have to do a tiny bit of work before dinner,' Dad says.

I feel a surge of disappointment. Dad's idea of a tiny bit of work is everyone else's idea of a huge great chunk of work. At least he's not like Jason, just hanging around all the time like he doesn't even know how to work hard, but still, I can't help slumping.

'Why don't you give the girls their presents from Paris, Lisa?' Dad says, as he heads into the study.

I'm not so disappointed anymore. Lisa might not be very good at cooking, but she's *really* good at choosing gifts.

'The presents are in our bedroom,' Lisa says. 'Want to come up?'

Romy and I follow Lisa, and I can tell that Romy is excited too because she actually moves faster than a snail for once.

Lisa and Dad's bedroom is upstairs. There's hardly ever any reason to go up there since it's just their bedroom and an ensuite, so I've forgotten how amazing it is.

It's huge. The carpet is cream with black, curved lines running through it. The cover on their king-sized bed is black, which might not look so good except for the cream and red cushions positioned perfectly against the headboard. I have no idea how they do it, but there's not so much as a wrinkle in the quilt cover. There's a red armchair in one corner, and you can just glimpse the city through shimmery, see-through curtains. There's nothing lying around that shouldn't be there.

'Sit on the bed, girls,' Lisa says.

Romy and I look at each other and I know we're thinking the same thing. We're going to crinkle the quilt cover. We sit lightly, our feet touching the carpet.

'So, Romy. You first,' Lisa says.

We watch as Lisa opens the door to her walk-in wardrobe. Everything in there seems to be colour-coded.

Mum's room couldn't be more different. She doesn't have a walk-in robe or an ensuite, or anything flashy at all. She has loads of paintings on the walls and clothes tossed over her chair and a rainbow quilt cover. But the funny thing is, if I had to choose my favourite bedroom, I'd say Mum's. It's cosier. It also has Jason in it half the time, though. I *so* don't want to think about that.

'Here you are, Romy,' Lisa says, giving her a box. Lisa slips off her shoes and leans back against the headboard.

Romy opens the box. Inside is a pair of black boots with wedge heels. 'Oh my god,' Romy breathes. 'These are awesome!'

Romy's school shoes are off and the boots are on in about two seconds.

'They fit perfectly!' she squeals. 'You knew my size?'

'I checked with Diana,' Lisa says. I can tell that Lisa is rapt that Romy loves the shoes. It sort of loosens Lisa up.

It's strange to think that Lisa and Mum have had a conversation about Romy's shoe size. I've only ever heard them talk about arranging visits and school work and uniforms and stuff. Mum keeps those conversations pretty short. And since I'm normally with Mum when she's on the phone with Lisa, I often see her rolling her eyes as though talking with Lisa is a real bore.

Romy struts around the room, kicking her legs up so she can see the boots better. She goes to the full-length mirror for a better look.

'I look *amazing*,' she says in a funny voice, doing kissy lips at her reflection.

Lisa laughs and it's really funny. I've heard her laugh before, but this isn't her normal, polite little chuckle. It's more like a snort. I think Mum might like Lisa better if she heard that snort.

'Don't even think about it, Hazel,' Romy says, doing another lap around the bed.

I giggle because I *am* thinking about how I could wear a few pairs of socks and then the boots might even fit me.

'Now to you, Hazel,' Lisa says with a big smile. 'Your dad and I had big discussions about your gift.'

'Really?' I say. 'Why?'

'Well, he wanted to get you something from the toy department, and I said you were getting a bit old for stuffed animals,' she says. 'So in the end, we compromised. Or maybe we doubled up.'

Lisa gets two presents from her wardrobe. The first present is wrapped in tissue paper and when I unwrap it I see it's one of those super-wrinkly dogs. It's *so* adorable. The fur is soft and shiny and his eyes look almost real and I can't help giving him a hug even though Lisa is right, I'm probably too old for this kind of thing.

'He's so cute. Thanks, Lisa,' I say warmly.

I lay him on my lap and I'm trying to decide between Albert and Winston for his name when Lisa hands me the second present. This one is in a shiny black bag with the name of a store in silver writing. The bag has little rope handles. Inside is a box. Lisa and Romy are both dead quiet as I open it.

Inside is the most beautiful bottle of perfume I've ever seen.

'Wow,' I say, and I can't think of anything better to say.

I've never owned anything like this before. The bottle is amazing. It's heavy glass with a long, curved gold neck and a glass ball on top. It looks like a genie bottle or something.

'It's sophisticated, don't you think?' Lisa says, looking at me closely.

Romy's eyes are like saucers. 'It's J'adore!' she says.

I know she's talking about a brand name and, to be honest, I've never heard of it. But it's clear from Romy's expression that she has, and that it's special.

Lisa unscrews the lid for me and squirts one short spray on each of my wrists. 'Now, wait for twenty seconds before you smell it,' she says.

We can't last twenty seconds, though. We're smelling my wrists after about five.

'That smells so fantastic,' Romy says, all dreamy and

jealous even though she has a fabulous pair of boots.

'I think it's the right scent for you, Hazel,' Lisa agrees. 'It's sophisticated but it's still young and fresh.'

I like Lisa at this moment more than I've ever liked her before. It's as though she's realised something that my own mum hasn't. That I'm ready to be *mature* with stuff like this. It's nice that at least she and Romy know! Plus, it's kind of funny how Romy keeps trying to spray her own wrist and I keep grabbing the bottle back.

'Well,' Romy says, 'I *might* consider renting these out,' she points to her boots, 'for a few sprays of J'adore.'

It's so nice to have something Romy wants for once.

'I'll think about it,' I say.

Romy holds out her hands, squints her eyes and wiggles her fingers. It's a threat. It means that she's thinking about tickle-torturing me.

'Okay, okay,' I giggle. 'I'll let you have a spray.'

Romy holds her wrists out to me but I race past her and charge out of the room, the perfume safely in my hands.

'If I feel like it!' I yell over my shoulder, heading towards Dad's study to find my tickle-torture protector.

Six

By the time Romy and I have finished breakfast the next morning, Dad and Lisa have left for work. They always leave early, which Romy and I love because it makes us feel all grown-up, being in their beautiful apartment on our own. We eat a second round of breakfast then end up doing our teeth together. We can do that at Dad and Lisa's because there are two sinks in the bathroom.

'Let's 'ave a spray ov 'erfume,' Romy says, her mouth full of toothpaste froth. She spits into the sink. 'Please.'

'Okay,' I say.

I fetch the bottle and allow Romy a squirt on each wrist. Because it's my perfume, I give myself four. Two on my wrists and two on my neck.

V

At school I feel a bit different to how I normally do. A bit more grown-up.

I'm getting my lunch out of my locker when Edi calls out to me.

'Haze, come down to the tree with me?' she asks.

Olympia and Jess have gone to the library because they have an assignment due after lunch.

I grimace. 'Um ...' I say.

The tree is a hangout for kids in the year above us. We don't belong there.

'Haze, you *have* to,' Edi urges. 'For me? It's *Thursday*!'

I know what Edi's getting at. Archie doesn't have soccer practice on Thursdays, so he'll probably be there.

'I'm *dying* to see him,' Edi moans. 'Please, please, please, please?'

'All right,' I sigh.

The only other time I've been down to the tree I felt really awkward, like I'd gatecrashed or something. But Edi doesn't care about stuff like that so I won't either. I hope.

'Oh my god,' Edi says as we get closer to where the others are all standing around, chatting. 'Just look at him. He's so hot!'

I look up at Archie. Edi's right, I guess. He is hot. He has olive skin and sort of emerald-green eyes, which is a pretty cool combo. Plus, he's muscly and he shaves. But I can't help thinking he *knows* he's cute. It somehow makes him less good-looking. Plus, he's obsessed with soccer, which is super boring. He's obviously talking about soccer right now, as I see him doing pretend kicks with a few other guys. Three of his mates watch and laugh, one slapping him on the back.

There's a fourth guy there, too. I know his name is Leo. I've seen him around school before and noticed his cute smile. He seems different to the others. He's tall and has curly hair, and he's leaning with his back against the tree, not being as slappy and cheery.

There are three girls from Archie's year who are sitting on the bench seat nearby, watching the boys too. I'm pretty sure that Archie is looking over at Edi. The rumours about him liking Edi must be true.

Edi and I haven't been there for long when Archie makes his way over to us. The girls on the bench seat follow him with their eyes. It makes me feel awkward, but Edi doesn't seem to notice. She looks like she belongs here.

'Hi,' Archie says, and I have to admit it's pretty cute. He's talking to the grass, like he can't look directly at Edi. He seems nervous.

'Hi, Archie,' Edi replies.

I say hi too, but I'm pretty sure Archie doesn't hear me. Edi tucks some hair behind her ears, both sides, and I swear she looks even better than she did a second ago because more of her beautiful face is showing.

It's funny watching Archie with Edi. I can almost see him melt as he looks at her. Everyone's watching them now. His mates are laughing and I reckon they can see what I see. The bench girls, though, are straight-faced and staring. I try to block them out.

'Um, ah, I am having an, um … a party,' Archie says. 'Next Saturday. I mean this Saturday. As in, this weekend.'

'Oh yeah?' Edi says, all casual, like she's talking to just anyone and not Archie de Souza.

'Yeah,' Archie confirms. 'So I was just wondering, um, ah, if you'd, um, like to come?'

'Sure,' Edi says without missing a beat. 'Can I bring my friends?'

My heart is racing now, even though Edi is obviously in complete control. I'm not sure I want to go to Archie's party. I know that kids in that year hook up all the time.

He looks worried. 'Um, it's invitation only and, um, I'm not really allowed to have …'

As Archie muddles through a speech about his mum and dad not wanting the party to be too huge, I hear footsteps behind me. I'm about to turn around, but before I get a chance, two hands clamp over my eyes. I know straight away who it is. Nick loves this game. It's sort of an awkward time, but the thing is, Nick doesn't understand about awkward times, so I have to play along.

I normally say about ten random names before I get

to his. When I finally guess it's Nick, it makes him really happy.

But today, the hands pull away quickly.

'You STINK, Hazel!' Nick says, really loudly.

I turn around, but Nick has taken a step backwards and he's shaking his hands in front of his chest like he does when he gets upset.

'Why do you STINK?'

The girls on the bench are all laughing and whispering behind their hands. Archie steps back from Nick, pulling Edi with him as though he can't wait to get away.

I wish I'd gone a bit easier on the perfume this morning. I wish the ground would open up and swallow me. Everyone probably thinks I've farted or something. I'm not sure what to do. I know Nick needs help to calm down, but I also know that if I'm the one who tries it, with my *stink* and all, he'll probably freak out even more.

'Hey, Nick,' says a soothing voice. I look up and see Leo walking towards us. 'It's okay, mate.' He puts his arm around Nick's shoulder and gives him a smile.

Next thing I know, Leo is leaning towards me and

taking a sniff. He still has his arm around Nick's shoulder. It's so weird, but my neck tingles where he sniffs, and it keeps on tingling even after he's stepped back.

He straightens up and smiles at me. He's not exactly hot, but there's something about him that's really nice. His brown eyes sort of scrunch up when he smiles, and his curly brown hair is all cute and messy.

I don't have a clue what my face is doing. I probably look like a rabbit in the spotlight.

'She's just wearing perfume, Nick,' Leo says gently.

Nick's hands have slowed down, but he's still not very calm. 'I like Hazel's *normal* smell,' Nick protests.

I grimace. I didn't even know I *had* a normal smell. Now everyone will know that at least Nick thinks I do. I feel the blood rush back to my cheeks. I'm seriously embarrassed, but Nick wouldn't understand that either. So, even though I'm blushing, I manage to say something to him.

'I can wash off the smell, Nick. It will go away.'

Nick nods. He slips out from under Leo's arm and walks away. That's another thing with Nick. He can be really upset one minute, and fine the next. He seems fine now. He's even stopped to catch a ball on the basketball court. He's interrupted a game and I see a guy waving his hands about for Nick to return the ball. Nick is grinning as he passes it back.

'You actually smell really good, Hazel.'

The tingle I felt in my neck turns into a shiver and runs down my back.

I can't think of a single thing to say. Leo just smiles that cute smile and walks back over to the boys. But I've got that sentence on replay in my mind.

You actually smell really good, Hazel. You actually smell really good, Hazel. You actually —

'How cool is this?' Edi says, breaking the cycle. 'Archie said I can bring *one* friend. I think that guy Leo must like you and he must've said something to Archie because then Archie said I should bring you. So, it's you and me, Hazel. We're going to Archie de Souza's party! You'll come, won't you?'

I nod and try not to grin like an idiot.

I think I've just changed my mind about going to Archie's party and the reason begins with an L.

V

'That's sooo unfair,' Olympia moans when we meet her and Jess at the lockers.

'Are you *sure* we can't come?' Jess adds. 'I've got *nothing* on this weekend. It's going to be so boring!'

'Sorry, guys,' Edi says. 'I did try, but it's invitation only.'

'Well, I know why *you're* invited, Edi,' Olympia says and the way she says it makes me stiffen. 'But how come *Hazel* gets to go?' She turns to me. 'No offence, Hazel.'

Now I feel really awkward. It's like Olympia is telling me I've jumped the queue. As though she thinks that number seventeen is pushing in ahead of number eight. I wonder if she'd be like this if Jess was going to Archie's party instead of me? I doubt it. Even though Jess is number eight and below Olympia too, I think she'd be *nicer* about it.

And the fact is, I'm pretty sure I only got the invitation because I was there with Edi. Still, if it was Olympia who was invited, I don't think I'd be like this with her. Actually, I'm sure I wouldn't be.

Normally I get all quiet and worried when Olympia is being mean, but this time she's making me mad. I'm just about to ask her what she means by the comment when Edi answers.

'You guys have to think of it like this,' she says, 'Hazel and I got the invitation *this time.* But this is just the start of things. If *we* get to be friends with Archie and the others, then pretty soon we'll be able to include both of you. It's just a matter of time.'

She's clever, Edi. She's definitely a girl with plans. I wouldn't have thought of that angle. I can see the idea sinking in for Olympia and Jess too.

'You really think so?' Olympia asks.

'Yep,' Edi says, nodding firmly.

'And you'll fill us in on *everything* that happens? Every tiny detail?' Jess asks.

'Definitely,' I say. 'Every little detail.' I direct it at Jess because I'm still a bit mad at Olympia.

'It'll be like having *spies* there to report back,' Jess says. She nudges Olympia. 'Come on, Limps. At least we'll get all the party goss.'

Olympia shrugs. I can tell she's still not over the moon that I'm going to Archie's party and she's not. But it does look like the idea of getting the party goss is making her feel better.

She gives me a friendly nudge like the one Jess just gave her.

'Every little detail, Hazel?' she says. When she smiles at me it feels like she's forgiven me for queue jumping or whatever she thinks I've done. Cold to hot. I make myself smile back, but honestly, it always seems like she could swing back to cold any minute and it drives me nuts. I wish I could see inside her mind and find out, once and for all, what she thinks of me.

'Every little detail, Olympia,' I promise.

Even though I'm weighed down with my overnight bag and my schoolbag, I feel like I'm floating home rather than walking. Thursday nights are family nights, which means, for us, no boys allowed. Maybe Mum and I will be able to have a proper talk this time. Maybe, when I tell her about being invited to a party from the year above, she might finally get that I'm growing up and then we might even be able to have the period talk again, but a better one this time.

There's weird music floating though our house when I open the front door. Whale calls with clanging cymbal noises in-between. I can't believe people like this kind of stuff. Every time the cymbals clang I feel jumpy.

I dump my bag in my room and head through. Mum's checking her emails on her laptop in the lounge room.

'Hi, buddy,' Mum says.

She must've caught the word from Jason, because she's never called me that before. I didn't know words were contagious, not for someone Mum's age anyway. Obviously bad music is too. I sneak a quick peek at Dad on the mantelpiece. He would *hate* this music.

'Hey, Mum,' I say, raising my eyebrows at the music.

'It's relaxing, Haze,' she says, closing the lid of her laptop. 'How was your father's?'

Mum never mentions Lisa unless she has to.

I'm about to answer when Romy appears from her

bedroom. She hasn't wasted any time getting the boots on. She looks good in her tunic dress, tights and boots. She knows it too. She catwalks around the lounge room. I wonder if I could convince her to let me wear that whole outfit to Archie's party.

'What do you think, Mum?' she asks, landing a boot on the couch next to Mum. 'I can't believe that Dad and Lisa got them. Thanks for giving them my size. I *love* them.'

'Mmm,' Mum says. There's a battle of expressions on her face, like she's trying to be positive but she doesn't want to be. Mum gets weird when Dad and Lisa buy us expensive stuff. 'They're … nice, Romy.'

Romy leans down and gives Mum a hug. She's good like that. Mum's face is way softer after the hug.

'Show her what you got, Hazel,' Romy says.

I nick back down the hallway to my room to get the perfume and the dog. When I come back into the lounge room, I hold out the beautiful bottle and Winston. Mum's face reverts to the battle zone.

'Well, I'm glad *someone* has money to burn,' she says, glaring at the perfume.

I try to ignore the dig. Mum shouldn't say stuff like that about Dad and Lisa, as though us not having much money is their fault.

'He's cute, Haze,' she says. I hand her Winston and she pats him like he's a real dog and I think that might be the end of the conversation, but there's more. 'But that perfume costs a fortune,' she says. She shakes her head. 'Ridiculous,' she mutters, 'for a thirteen-year-old.'

'Thirteen and four months,' I point out, putting the perfume in my pocket.

'I don't know what gets into Lisa's head,' Mum says.

'Gee, I don't know,' I say sarcastically. 'Maybe Lisa thinks I deserve some beautiful perfume? Maybe she thinks that I'm not a kid anymore.' This conversation is happening all wrong – again. You'd think she'd want to try a bit harder this time. 'Maybe I'll ask Lisa to take me to the doctor, since she's the only one who gets it!'

Romy's phone rings and she uses it as an excuse to go to her room. Mum rubs the bridge of her nose with two fingers, as if talking about this stuff has given her a massive headache. But she pats the seat next to her on the couch.

A harp has joined in with the whales and cymbals. If Mum has a headache, I reckon this stupid music is the real cause.

I sit down. Winston is between us.

'Okay, Hazel, okay,' she says. 'I understand that you're worried about not getting your period yet.' She sighs a long sigh and pats Winston. 'I honestly don't think there's anything to worry about, but I'll book an appointment for you if it makes you feel better. There's a lovely female doctor at the clinic now. I'll do it, okay?'

'Okay,' I say, and it feels good that she's finally acknowledging the problem. I wish she would stop right there but she doesn't.

'The thing is,' she continues, and she's interrupted by a couple of long whale groans. 'The thing is,' she repeats, 'I really think you're almost there. I mean, you're definitely having mood swings.'

It's such an annoying thing for Mum to say. *If I've been moody,* I think to myself, *it's because everything has changed around here. If I've been moody, then the reason has dreadlocks and wears paint-splattered trackie dacks.*

But I squash down my feelings. Because she doesn't get it. At all.

'You know, the timing really doesn't matter, Hazel,' Mum continues. 'Whether you get your period right now or in a few months' time is no big deal. All that matters is that you're happy being yourself, whatever stage you're at. I just hope you're not hurrying to be something you're not.'

She says it like she's just solved the Problem Of The Universe in a few sentences. She smiles at me as if she's Buddha or something.

She sits up straighter, clearly changing the topic. 'Now, I hope you don't mind, hon, but Jason's getting off work early. He's going to pick up the pizzas on the way over.'

She might as well have slapped me.

There's another whale noise, and suddenly everything just bursts out of me.

'You know what?' I say. 'I actually don't care that Jason's coming over on our special girls' night, because he might as well be here, even when he isn't. You tell me to be happy being myself. But what about you? *You're* being someone you're not. I can't believe you're even listening to this crap whale music. This is Jason's taste in music, not yours.'

I get up and turn off the iPod while it all keeps spewing out of me. 'One minute you say you're happy with just me and Romy. The next, you're hanging out all the time with him and you're listening to his stupid music and you're calling me *buddy* and you're letting him take over our lives and you're changing so much it's like having a completely different mum. I don't think you even care about me and Romy anymore. It's like all you care about is him. And then you have a go at Lisa for buying me perfume? Well, at least Lisa has noticed I'm growing up!'

I hear the front door open. I can't believe it. The Feral has his own key?

Mum's staring at me, looking shocked. I don't even know the next bit is coming until I say it. 'Maybe I should just go and live with Dad and Lisa.' It comes out quietly. As soon as it comes out I feel really shaky.

I grab Winston, not looking at Mum, and storm off to my room. I walk straight past Jason and ignore the yummy-smelling pizzas and him calling hello like everything's fine.

In my room I snuggle under the covers in the dark, trying to ignore my rumbling tummy. I don't want to live with Dad and Lisa. I like it there, but *this* is my home. I look up at the ceiling. Years ago, Mum helped me put up glow-in-the-dark stickers of the solar system. Stars and planets and the moon. Most of them have lost their glow now. It's a bit like me and Mum. Everything between us was fine. Bright. Now it's like all the glow has faded.

It's been ages and Mum hasn't even come to check on me. I can hear plates clanking in the kitchen, then the TV is switched on.

Finally, there are footsteps coming down the hallway. Mum opens the door and just stands there for a moment.

'Hazel,' she whispers, 'do you want to come out and get some pizza? We're about to watch the DVD too.'

I sit up. Mum leans against the doorframe and sighs. I stare at her. It's so weird. She's right there in front of me, but I miss her.

'Hazel,' she says slowly, 'storming off all the time won't solve anything.'

I hug Winston to my chest.

'I'm tired,' I say. It's the truth. I am tired. Of everything.

'Okay, Hazel.' She sighs and shakes her head. Like she's given up on me. She walks away.

I wait until I hear the DVD start. I sneak up the hallway and peer around the corner. Mum and Jason are on the couch and Romy is in her favourite position, lying on the carpet with her head propped up on her elbows.

They don't even notice me go past.

I get a couple of slices of cold pizza from the kitchen and take the plate back to my room. I only eat one.

I wish Mum would come back into my room. I wish she'd come and give me a hug and say she's sorry about Jason coming over on our girls' night. Then I'd say sorry about saying I'd go and live with Dad and Lisa, and then we'd talk about stuff like we used to.

But she doesn't come back. I cuddle Winston and stare at the ceiling.

I haven't even told her about the party.

Seven

'Want to borrow something?' Edi says, opening her wardrobe.

It's Saturday – party day – and we're in Edi's bedroom, in her actual house for once. It reminds me a bit of my bedroom at Dad and Lisa's house. It's really neat and there are no pictures on the walls and definitely no babyish stars on the ceiling.

I groan. 'Do I look terrible?' I ask. Part of me wishes I'd brought the outfit to show everyone at our caravan meeting last night. I'm pretty sure Olympia would have told me if she thought it sucked. She's been okay for the last couple of days, but I think that's partly because I've tried to back off whenever Edi's around so that Olympia can have her to herself.

But Jess would be too nice to tell me if the outfit was terrible, and Edi finds it so easy to get her look right that I think she assumes it's that way for everyone. It has taken her about five minutes to look more amazing than usual.

She switches on her hair straightener and snaps it at me like a crocodile. 'I didn't mean it like that,' she says. 'You look great. Just let me do your hair.'

I'm not sure she's right about that. Romy has let me borrow her boots. Not even as a trade for perfume. She just let me wear them. I think it's got something to do with her feeling bad about what's going on between me and Mum. But she didn't feel bad enough to let me wear her tunic, so I'm wearing them with my skinny jeans and a black singlet top. My feet feel hot in all the pairs of socks I'm wearing as I walk over to Edi's dressing table.

I can see both of us in the mirror as she takes portions of my hair and irons out the kinks. I definitely don't look as good as she does. Her top is pale yellow with a few spangles here and there and it looks incredible against her caramel-toned skin.

'If Archie asks me to go out with him, I'm going to say yes.' Edi nods at her reflection in the mirror like it's actually happening in her head right now. Whatever it is that's playing out in her imagination must be pretty interesting because she stays on one section of my hair for so long that steam rises out.

'Um, time to move on?' I say, and then, because that sounds like I'm being serious, I continue. 'As in, I know you're burning for him, but really, leave my hair out of it.'

There's a little shudder down my spine as we laugh. It's a nervous shudder as well as an excited one. As usual, Edi is twenty million steps ahead of me. Which is fine if you're Edi, number one 'hot girl', beautiful and confident and totally ready to go to a party where everyone will be older than us.

Maybe not so fine when you're number seventeen and not so beautiful or so confident and not even getting your period. Still.

I wonder if I'll get to talk to Leo. I wonder if, possibly, maybe … just maybe, something might happen between *us*. It's a scary kind of wonder, but not bad scary somehow. I think of how kind he was to Nick down at the tree the other day and the wonder expands. A lot of people don't know how to handle Nick. They like to just avoid him. Not Leo. When I think about that, I think of how he leant in and sniffed my perfume and I get that tingly feeling all over again, even though he's not here!

You actually smell really good, Hazel. You actually …

Edi's dad is standing in the doorway. 'Edi? Now.'

'Hi, I'm Hazel,' I say, my *meeting the parents* smile on my face.

Edi's dad looks at me blankly for a moment before he says hello. Then I expect Edi to tell him to give us a few minutes. But neither of those things happen.

I guess I'm lucky that Edi's finished my hair because two minutes later we're in the car on the way to Archie's. It's so weird how her dad hardly says anything, except to say goodbye and arrange the pick-up time. Even Edi's really quiet when he's around.

'Is your dad okay?' I ask Edi when we get out of the car. 'Are you fighting or something?'

I haven't spoken to Edi or the others about what's going on at home, and it strikes me for the first time that maybe I should. Maybe Edi has stuff going on with her parents too, even if they're different problems to mine.

For a moment she looks un-Edi-like. Almost upset. 'That's what he's always like,' Edi replies.

Then she shakes her head as though she's shaking off whatever it is that's wrong with her dad and we walk to the front door.

'Ready?' Edi asks.

We stop and look at each other.

Please don't let me make an idiot of myself in there. I shrug and go cross-eyed.

'Nice look, Hazel,' she giggles. 'Perfect for the party.'

I know Edi gets that I'm trying to release the idiot inside me *before* I go in.

I can tell it's Archie's mum who opens the door. She's really big and round where Archie is tall and buff, but she has the same olive skin and green eyes.

'Hi, girls,' she says warmly. 'Don't you look lovely? Come in!'

We walk behind her down the hall. At the end of the hallway there's a kitchen that opens up into the lounge room. I try to spot Leo but it's hard to see what's going on because a smoke machine is making the room hazy. The music is loud, but I don't think anyone is dancing yet.

'Look, the poor loves are starving!' Archie's mum says, gesturing into the kitchen.

There's a group of guys huddled around the oven. They've got their backs to us but I can tell one of them is Archie.

'Hands off, garbage guts!' It's a female voice and it's familiar but I can't quite place it. Whoever it is must be crouching in front of the oven. 'Honestly, Archie, you're the biggest pig,' the voice comes again, followed by a giggle.

'Come on, Al. Be nice. It's my *birthday*,' Archie replies.

The someone stands up. It's Alice!

'Well, happy birthday. But hands off,' she says, slapping his hand away from the tray.

As soon as she puts the tray on the bench, Archie gets her in a headlock. It's *so* weird to watch. I would never have expected Alice to be here, but it's clear she's totally comfortable mucking around with one of the most popular guys in school. Edi and I are the ones who are kind of awkward, just standing there, watching and waiting for Archie to see us.

Archie spins around with Alice still in a headlock.

'Edi!' he says, loosening his grip on Alice. 'Hi. I didn't know you were here.' His face goes red.

I wonder if I'm invisible.

'Hi, Hazel,' Alice says, with a punch to Archie's sixpack.

Archie has that melting thing going on as he stares at Edi. He doesn't seem to even notice Alice's punch. Alice takes the opportunity to slip out of his grip and come over to me.

I must look a bit surprised.

'Old family friends,' Alice explains, pointing at Archie and his mum. 'Hi, Edi.'

It's nice that Alice has said hi to me before she said hi to Edi. Just for once, it's nice to be thought of first.

V

I can't really talk to anyone in the lounge room. The music is too loud. I hang with Edi and Alice and look around through the smoke. The girls who were on the bench when we went down to the tree are dancing together. They're pretty good and I'm glad not everyone's dancing because I wouldn't want anyone to see my lame dance moves.

'Where's Archie? I haven't seen him for *ages*,' Edi yells in my ear, making my eardrums buzz.

I point through the smoke haze to where Archie is talking to his soccer mates. It's funny, but every time Edi manages to get close to him, he seems to move somewhere else. My theory is he's avoiding her because he really likes her. Maybe he's worried about melting into a heap in front of everyone?

Edi takes off towards him. If Alice decides to follow her I'll be left standing by myself like a complete dork. I'm stressing about that possibility, so I start to say something to her. But then, I see Leo arriving. Finally.

He waves and starts walking over to me and Alice, and something weird happens inside my body, like there's a little helium balloon in my ribcage.

'Hi,' he says and then he leans in towards me just like he did at school, except this time he tilts his head to the side and he's so close I can feel his breath on my neck.

'Still driving the boys crazy?' he asks with that crinkly smile.

I have put a bit of perfume on for tonight. Just a little bit, though.

'Yeah, I've totally got the knack,' I reply. 'It's just one of my many talents.'

Leo's laugh floats over the top of the music. The helium balloon expands inside me. I feel like I might be lifted off the floor.

'This is Alice,' I say. 'Alice, Leo.' They say hi to each other, but when Leo talks again, he directs it to me.

'So, what other talents do you have, Hazel?' he asks.

'Well, I like horseriding and meeting people,' I say.

As soon as I say it, I feel cringy. I'm trying to act like the girls in those Miss Universe pageant thingies, but he probably won't get it. He'll probably just think I'm lame.

'And I suppose your goal in life is to end world hunger?' he says.

I laugh with relief. 'Yep. I'm going to get right onto that after the bikini parade,' I say. This time Leo's laugh is way louder and it feels amazing that he's totally got it, that he's got *me*, and I've made him laugh.

Alice laughs too, and it's only then I remember that there are others around me, that we're at Archie's party. I was in a Leo-bubble for a moment there.

I wouldn't mind going back into it, but one of the bench girls, Eliza, has come over.

'Truth or dare time, Leo,' she says. 'Basement.'

She doesn't even acknowledge that Alice and I are there, and I get the feeling I had down at the tree – that there are quite a lot of girls here who would prefer it if we weren't.

Eliza shakes her head, as though she's changed her mind. 'You girls can play too, I suppose,' she says. 'If you're up for it.'

She doesn't wait for an answer. She grabs Leo's hand and pulls him over to the stairs. Leo smiles at me over his shoulder as he gets dragged away. I can see the back of Edi's head. She's going down to the basement too.

'I'm going to help Archie's mum in the kitchen,' Alice whispers. 'Wanna come?'

It's tempting. But Leo is down there and so is Edi and part of me doesn't want to miss out. I don't want it to seem like I'm not up for it.

V

The basement is pretty bare. The floor is concrete and there are a few beanbags around, but not enough for everyone. There's one of those giant old freezers and a sink in the corner. To the side, there's a big cupboard.

'In a circle, everyone!' Eliza orders.

I'm glad when Edi squashes in next to me on my right. The concrete feels hard and cold on my knees. Leo's on the other side of the circle, sitting cross-legged. I change my position from up on my knees to cross-legged and even though it's cold on my bum, I feel a bit more comfortable.

Eliza is the only one standing. She points to a guy a few

people to my left. I'm pretty sure you're supposed to spin a bottle or something to see who goes first, but I'm definitely not going to say anything about it.

'Truth or dare?' she asks.

'Truth is for gutless wonders,' the guy says. 'Dare!'

Eliza gets her iPhone out and shakes it. She looks at the screen and laughs before she reads it aloud.

'A random player soaks one of their socks in water and puts it in the freezer. After five rounds, you must take it out and suck it like an icy pole.'

There's a lot of laughter going around the circle. Especially when one of Archie's soccer friends, someone called Pezza, volunteers his sock.

'Had this on for three days in a row,' he says, taking a sock off and walking over to the sink. 'I reckon it'll be really tasty!' He fills the sock with water and opens the freezer, looking for a spot to put it. 'Will I put it on top of the meat or the ice-cream?'

'The meat!' a few people yell.

It's pretty funny. I laugh along with everyone. It would be gross to have to suck someone's sock, but it's a bit of a relief too. *Maybe the truth and dares will all be like this and not like hooking up and stuff?*

Everyone's still chatting and laughing when Eliza strikes again.

'We're going clockwise. So it's your turn, Bridget. Truth or dare?'

It hits me like a whack in the chest. If we're going clockwise, then I'm only two players off having a turn.

'After that,' Bridget laughs, 'I think I'll choose truth.'

Eliza shakes the iPhone again. 'If you were a boy, which girl here would you date?'

I'm stressing. After Bridget answers, there will only be one other person before it's *my* turn. I think of Alice, safely upstairs in the kitchen. If Edi wanted to get out of here, we could make up something so it wouldn't be too embarrassing. I give her leg a flick with my fingers and she looks at me, but it isn't a *let's get out of here* look. It's more of a *how fun is this?* look.

'Mmmm,' Bridget says, 'bit of a stupid question really. It implies that everyone is straight. Which may not be the case –'

'Jeez, Bridge,' says Eliza, 'we're not in class. We're not here to *analyse* the question. Just answer it, okay?'

The way she says it is mean, and it makes me think Eliza might be mean to everyone and not just to me, Edi and Alice. But that doesn't help much. I don't even really get what Bridget's on about. She doesn't *look* like she's gay. I mean, I'm not exactly sure what gay people look like. But maybe she is, or maybe she's just making a point. Does everyone else get what she's on about except for me?

It's all very confusing and it makes me feel even more like I want to escape.

'All right. She's the prettiest,' Bridget says, pointing to Edi. 'But I don't know what her personality is like.' She points to another girl. 'So I'll go with Leah,' she says.

Leah, a tall girl in the year above us, holds out two thumbs up.

'Next,' says Eliza, to the guy *right next to me*.

'Truth,' he says. 'I'm still freaking out about that sock. If Pezza says three days, think five or six. Believe me, I know.'

Everyone laughs again. When things settle, Eliza looks at her phone and says, 'Nelson, tell the group about your best and worst kissing experiences.'

'Ah,' he says like he's been let off the hook. 'Too easy. My best was when I was on holiday in Thailand.' He traces an hourglass shape in the air with his hands. 'She was tall and blonde and sexy –'

'And imaginary!' someone yells out and people laugh, but Nelson doesn't let that stop him.

'And she had the best lips ever. We were lying on the beach, side by side, and it was so hot and she just leant over and it was great. Ten out of ten.'

'And your worst kiss?' Eliza reminds him.

'It was at school, about two months ago. Her breath was gross and she slobbered. I give her zero out of ten.'

Some people are sort of twittering. I wonder if they know the girl he's talking about? It would be *so* horrible to be her if they did.

I wriggle my bum over closer to Edi and as far away from Nelson as I can go. My heart is beating so hard I'm sure the others will be able to hear it.

'All right,' Eliza says, shaking her phone already and looking at me.

'You,' she says to me. 'Truth or dare?'

Eight

Truth, dare? Dare, truth? The two words flick through my mind. I've been so worried about my turn I haven't had a chance to worry about which one I should pick. I breathe.

I have to pick dare, don't I? What if I got asked a question like the one Nelson got? Imagine if I got asked about my best and worst kissing experiences!

How would I answer that?

Oh, my best and worst are the same. In year five, Tyson Banks kissed me on the cheek and ran away.

It would be ... it would be like suicide. I'd rather suck a

smelly-sock icy pole than tell everyone that.

'You planning on answering anytime soon?' Eliza says, her hand on her hip.

I clear my throat. 'Dare.'

Edi pinches me on the thigh as though this is all really exciting.

Eliza looks down at the screen. 'Seven minutes in heaven,' she says.

A cheer goes up around the room. I have no idea what that means, but clearly everyone else does. I look over at Leo. He looks uncomfortable. Eliza rolls her eyes at my blank face, as though having to explain it to me is a pain.

'Go into a dark space for seven minutes with a boy.'

For a moment, I feel a twinge of excitement mixed up in my fear. Could I dare to choose Leo?

Eliza interrupts with bad news. 'With the boy closest to you,' she says.

Even though I've squished up as close as I can get to Edi, there's no question which boy is closest to me. It's Nelson. The one who told us all about his best kiss. And his worst.

'And you can just do … whatever,' Eliza finishes. She says 'whatever' really slowly, like she's suggesting something should happen in those seven minutes that I don't even want to think about.

Nelson gets up straight away. He holds out his hand and pulls me up. His hand's all sweaty.

I don't look over at Leo as Nelson leads me across the circle towards the cupboard. I can feel the extra socks in my boots and it's like a reminder that this situation is too big for me, the same way Romy's boots are.

I've already passed by Leo when I look back, but he's staring down at the concrete in front of him.

Nelson opens the cupboard door. It's pretty big, for a cupboard. But with all the mops and brooms and cleaning stuff it still feels tight.

When we're squeezed inside, Nelson closes the door behind us. It's dark, but at least there are shafts of light from the gap under the door so I can see his face. He leans back against the side of the cupboard.

I can hear the others outside getting on with the game.

'So,' Nelson says, peering over at me in the dark.

'What's your name?'

'Hazel.' I wonder if he can hear my heart thumping. I take a step backwards and trip on a dustpan and brush. He reaches out and grabs me around the waist. I know he's trying to steady me, but he doesn't need to keep his hands there after I've got my balance back. I think about pushing his hands away, but I don't.

'Nice name,' he says.

'Thanks,' I say, just to say something.

His hands are hot and sweaty against my singlet top.

'That's okay,' he says, sounding smug, like he's said something smart or romantic and he's made a *connection* with me. Which he hasn't. Does he honestly think no-one's ever told me Hazel is a nice name?

My mind flashes back to the talk I had with Leo earlier.

'Wanna hook up, Hazel?' Nelson asks next.

I wriggle out of his grip and side-step as far as I can go. I hear laughing coming from outside. Pezza's sock is out of the freezer. I wish I was out there to see it. I wish I was anywhere but here.

'Nervous, huh?' Nelson says. He's probably trying to be kind but he just sounds arrogant. 'Don't worry, Hazel. If you haven't done this before, I can break you in.'

I hold my breath. I'm not a horse. And I don't want to be broken in. Not by Nelson anyway. I *so* don't want my first kiss to be like this, in a broom cupboard with a guy like Nelson. Maybe if it was Leo I'd do it. But even then, I'm not sure. All I know is that I don't want to kiss this guy.

I try to send the vibe, but Nelson's not getting it. He dips his head towards me. There's nowhere for my feet to go, so I swivel my head to the side. He does a little face plant, all wet on my ear. It's so awkward. I can't believe it but I think he's going to give it a second go when there's a knock on the cupboard door.

'Guys? You in there?' comes Alice's voice. 'It's time to cut the cake.'

I *love* Alice. I can hear footsteps going up the stairs as everyone else heads back up, and Nelson finally moves away from me and leans against the cupboard door again.

My heart starts to settle down and I can breathe.

'Don't want to hook up, right?' Nelson says. *Genius.*

'Right,' I say, and then I feel like I have to soften it a bit. 'Sorry.'

Nelson shakes his head. 'Orright,' he says. 'Reckon we would have done seven minutes by now. And you're too young for me anyway.'

I wasn't too young for him a minute ago, but I'm definitely not going to argue. I'm just glad it's over.

He's just about to push open the door when he turns to me again. 'If anyone asks, just say we did, okay?'

'Yeah, sure,' I say quickly.

It seems like a good solution. I get to save my first kiss for someone else, and he gets to save face.

Nelson opens the cupboard door and we practically sprint up the stairs.

Archie is standing between his mum and Alice at the head of the table, and everyone's gathered around singing Happy Birthday. Well, the girls are singing. Most of the boys seem to be just moving their mouths.

Edi grabs my arm and pulls me away into the lounge room where we can be by ourselves.

'What happened?' she asks, flopping down on the couch and pulling me down with her. I think of the deal I made to Nelson. But I have to tell Edi what happened.

'It was sooo awkward, Edi,' I groan, putting my head into the back of the couch. 'He tried to kiss me.'

'So what did you do?'

'I turned my head at the last moment.'

I do a dramatic head-swivel to demonstrate, and Edi laughs like she doesn't think it was such a stupid move, which is a relief. Then she shakes her head and I think she's going to ask me more, but she doesn't.

'I chose dare,' she says.

'Oh! What was it?' I'm annoyed I missed Edi's turn.

'I had to choose a boy and sit on his lap for the next round.'

'At least you got to choose!' I say. 'So you chose Archie?'

'Of course,' she says, as though it's obvious. The thing is, if I got that dare I don't know if I could have even chosen Leo, because then everyone would think I like him. Which

I'm pretty sure I do, but I'm so not ready for everyone to know about it.

That stuff doesn't seem to bother Edi, but something is bothering her. She's frowning.

I can picture Edi sitting on Archie's lap. If it had been me, I'd probably be really uncomfortable and I'd look like an idiot. Not Edi.

'That's good, isn't it?' I offer, but I can tell *something's* not good.

'Yeah, but I wanted to stay there for the rest of the game. But when that round finished, that Eliza girl goes, *That round is over, Edi. You can get off Archie's lap now.*'

'Oh,' I say. I would've been relieved that she said that. Plus, I'm pretty sure Eliza wouldn't have a clue what *my* name is. In a way, I'd be flattered if I was on her radar enough for her to know who I am. But Edi doesn't seem to be thinking along those lines at all.

'So I get one lousy minute on Archie's lap and *nothing* else happens? And now it's just about time to go home. Dad's already texted. We have to be out the front in five minutes.'

I lean back on the couch. If I had got Edi's dare and I was brave enough to sit on Leo's lap, that would have totally been amazing. It's weird that she's younger than me and I'm always the one behind her with no clue how to catch up.

People start coming into the lounge room. First there's Eliza and the other girls. Then Leo walks in.

I look at him and I hope to god he's going to come over to the couch, and that he knows that nothing happened with Nelson and me in the cupboard. I try to send the *nothing happened* message to him through my eyes. But it doesn't look like it's reached him. He doesn't even return my smile. He just turns around and walks out of the room.

I don't see him again before we go home.

Nine

'Why was *Alice* invited to Archie's party?' Olympia asks.

It's Monday morning, and we're at our lockers. Edi and I spent ages yesterday on Facebook, messaging Jess and Olympia and filling them in about the party. We told them about Alice being there and my dare and Edi's dare. But even so, they still want more details.

'She's a family friend,' I explain. 'Apparently she's known Archie and his whole family forever.'

'That's so weird,' Jess says. 'You wouldn't expect that, would you? Like, people don't know that my family knows the Kingstons. Mum used to work with Eliza's mum and – '

'So, why didn't you kiss Nelson?' Olympia interrupts Jess, who was definitely gearing up for one of her long stories. 'Not even one little peck?' she prompts. 'Even if I didn't really like him, I reckon I would have done it just for the practice.'

'Yeah, kind of like kissing training,' Jess adds.

I get a funny feeling in my tummy. Jess keeps talking, but I'm not listening. Maybe I should have just done it? Like it was no big deal. Like it was kissing training. God knows, I need the practice more than anyone.

'Hazel didn't hook up with Nelson because Leo was there and she likes him better,' Edi explains for me, and it makes me feel better, but I'm not sure it's totally true.

I don't think I would have wanted to hook up with Nelson even if Leo wasn't there.

'Oh my god, you like *Leo*, Hazel?' Jess practically yells.

'Sshhh!' I say quickly, looking around to see who might have heard her.

To my horror a few of Archie's soccer mates are walking down the hallway.

I'm pretty sure that even if Leo did like me at the start of the party, he didn't like me by the end of it. And anyway, I don't want any rumours to fly around that make me look like an idiot. Well, like even *more* of an idiot.

V

I don't see the girls again until lunchtime. We meet up at our lockers, like we usually do.

'What's going on over there?' Olympia asks, pointing with her half-eaten muesli bar.

I look over to where Olympia is pointing. There's a bunch of people gathered around the noticeboard. It could just be an excursion notice or a call for auditions for the school play or something like that. But I have a funny feeling about it. It's like there's a block of lead sitting in my tummy. The four of us walk over.

There's a new hot list for our year up there. On the noticeboard. For everyone to see.

Edi is still number one.

I notice my own name really quickly, because there's

something written next to it. I've dropped down to number twenty-three. And next to my name, in capital letters, there's this:

FRIGID. MIGHT BE HOTTER
WHEN SHE GROWS UP.

'Come on, Haze,' says Edi. 'Don't look.' She sounds angry.

'Yeah, come away,' says Jess or Olympia. I don't even know who's talking because everything is churning. My head. My stomach. I can't move. I just stare at the writing.

I can feel tears spring up in my eyes. The list is wobbly through them, but I manage to pick out Alice's name. She's got my old position. Number seventeen.

The girls have to practically carry me to the toilets. I'm too stunned to even cry properly. I'm shaking as I slump onto a toilet seat. Edi puts her arms around me.

'Haze, it's just a stupid list,' she says.

'I'm going to find out who wrote that stuff and I'm going to kick them in the gonads,' Jess says.

But I already know who wrote it.

'Nelson,' I say, looking around at my friends.

He's obviously found out that I didn't stick to our deal. This is his revenge. And it's the perfect revenge. My life is over.

'I'm going to get a giant fire hose and spray him until he squeals,' Olympia adds. They mean well but it doesn't help. It's probably gone around the whole school by now.

It's so *humiliating*. It burns inside me and I can feel it burning on the outside too. My cheeks are flushed hot.

Everyone will know that I couldn't just shut my eyes and kiss a random boy in a closet. And I probably wouldn't even be ready to kiss the boy I like. Now everyone will think that there's something wrong with me. Actually, maybe they'll *know* it. They'll know that I'm way behind everyone else. They'll probably even work out that I haven't got my period yet.

The toilet door swings open. It's Alice, just like the last time. This time, though, she marches straight over to us. She's holding up the list between her thumb and forefinger, as though it's a dirty tissue. I look at Alice blankly, wondering how she got it.

'I ripped it off the noticeboard,' she says, as though she

can read my thoughts. 'And if they put it up again, I'll rip it down. As many times as it takes, Hazel.'

The girls are quiet. I am too. I haven't seen Alice like this, not since we started high school anyway. It's like being angry has made her confident again.

'You did the right thing at the party, Hazel,' she says. 'Anyone with half a brain could figure out that Nelson only wrote this stuff because you wouldn't kiss him. Why would you want to kiss a toad like him anyway?'

She looks around at us all. 'It's just *rubbish,*' she goes on. 'He walks around, scoring girls out of ten like he's the judge of everything? If you'd kissed him, he probably would have given you a score, just like he did Phoebe. Zero!'

Phoebe must have been the girl he talked about kissing on the oval. For a moment, I think about how horrible it is that he scored her kiss out of ten. But what he wrote about me is probably even worse.

It's weird because suddenly it's anger that's bubbling inside me instead of shame. Maybe I'm catching the feeling from Alice. The anger is almost kicking out the humiliation. Almost.

'Archie reckons Nelson's always going on about this girl he met on holidays,' Alice continues, 'but nobody's seen a photo of her so she probably doesn't even *exist*. Archie doesn't even like Nelson, but he had to invite him to the party because he's on the soccer team and the rest of the team were coming.'

Alice has been looking at me the whole time she's been talking. Now that she's paused, it's like she's realised that Edi, Jess and Olympia are there too. Edi is staring at Alice, and I reckon she's probably wondering how Alice got to be so close to Archie that she knows this stuff, but of course Alice doesn't know that.

I want to say something. Alice has actually gone up in the ranking but it's clear she doesn't care. This obviously matters more to her.

'Thanks, Alice,' I say. And I start crying for real this time. I'm not quite sure why, but it might be the relief and also realising how stupid it all is. 'What you did was really ... *brave*.'

She shakes her head as she looks at me. 'What *you* did was really brave, Hazel. You didn't let Nelson push you into something you didn't want to do.'

I hadn't thought of it like that. But maybe Alice is right. Maybe not kissing Nelson *was* brave in a weird way. Just thinking about it like this makes me feel stronger, but I don't get much time to think about it because Edi reaches out and takes the list from Alice.

'This,' she says as she rips the paper in half, 'is wrong. Even without the nasty things about Hazel, it's wrong. Why should we let a bunch of boys *rate* us?'

She tears the list into quarters. Then Jess takes it and rips it and hands the rest to Olympia. Limps holds it high in the air. Her eyes are wide as she looks at me.

'Whoever wrote this must be a complete loser, Hazel. Stuff him! You are smart. You are funny. And you're quite pretty in your own way.'

I shake my head as Olympia starts ripping. The last bit was kind of weird. I'm not sure about the 'quite pretty' thing. And I'll probably never really know which way is up with her, but right now she's got my back and it's enough.

Olympia hands the remnants of the list to me and it feels good to tear it to shreds. By the time we've all finished, the list is like pieces of confetti strewn all over the floor.

'Come on, Haze,' Edi says. 'We'll all walk out there together.'

I try to breathe deeply. I feel better. Not totally better. I'm still embarrassed about what was on the list and I'm worried about facing everyone. I still feel that lump of lead in my tummy. But at least we're all going to stick together and I won't have to face the world alone.

Edi moves towards the door and Jess and Olympia follow her. Alice hesitates, like she's not sure if she's supposed to come out with us. I stay behind with her.

'Thanks, Alice,' I say again. 'I don't know what I would have done –'

Edi interrupts me by poking her head through the door. 'Are you two coming or what?' she smiles.

Alice smiles back. I can tell she's happy that Edi is including her, though I'm not sure how Jess and Olympia will feel about it.

Alice and I head towards the door together.

Alice puts her hand on my arm to stop me. 'Oh yeah. With all this going on I almost forgot to tell you,' she grins at me. 'Leo said he's glad that you didn't hook up with Nelson. And he likes you,' she says the last bit in a whisper.

I grin back at her, feeling a little flash of pleasure.

I feel stronger now. Strong enough, with my support crew, to walk out and face everyone.

Ten

I keep pretty quiet over the next couple of days. I don't go down to the tree. I don't see Leo. I actually don't want to, not yet anyway. I'm pretty sure I do like him, but there's too much going on in my head to figure out my feelings properly.

At lunchtimes, we hang out in our own little zone on the grass slope at the side of the basketball courts. Alice sometimes comes too. Other times, she hangs out with Leni, Sophie and Anya. I notice, for the first time, how the other group of girls gets really animated when she joins them. And when she's with us, she really does add something different. Plus, she seems really happy. Like drifting between groups is about fitting in lots of different places rather than not fitting in at all. It makes me wonder whether I was even right to feel sorry for her in the first place. Maybe it's just me who needs to belong to one group of friends?

On Monday, the day the list went up, there were definitely kids whispering and looking at me. Yesterday, there were only whispers once and I'm not even sure they were talking about me.

But I must still be stressed because when I wake up on Tuesday morning, I have an ache in the base of my spine. I think about not going to school at all but part of me knows I need to tough it out. I need that list to be yesterday's news, and I need everyone to see me walking around like it doesn't matter. I drag myself out of bed and wander into the kitchen to get breakfast. Mum's in the shower and Romy's in her room getting ready.

I notice there's a little card for a doctor's appointment stuck up on the fridge under a magnet. It's for next

Thursday. More than a week away. I mean, it's good that she's done it at last, but it clearly shows how *urgent* Mum thinks me not getting my period is.

I don't say anything about it when Mum comes into the kitchen. We're all in a major hurry like most mornings anyway.

I only get through the day by hanging out at sick bay for a couple of hours. By the time I meet Romy at the bus stop after school, I feel okay again. I get the window seat and Romy sits next to me.

'I've got, like, three hours of homework,' she complains. 'You'd reckon the teachers would sort themselves out so they know what we're getting for each …' She trails off at what must be a very funny look on my face. 'What's wrong?' she asks.

I'm just sitting there, on the bus, on the way to Dad and Lisa's. It's like every other Wednesday afternoon, but there's something very weird happening. I'm pretty sure I can feel it. A trickle, a wetness, in my undies.

'I think I've got it,' I whisper to Romy. Even as I say it, I think I must be making a mistake. If I *ever* get my period, surely I'll get it somewhere special, somewhere memorable. Not on the bus to Dad and Lisa's.

Romy's head jerks back in surprise. 'Wow,' she whispers, grabbing my hand in excitement. 'Finally! Are you okay? Do you feel okay?'

Just as she's talking, I feel it again. There's definitely something going on down there. If it soaks through my undies and onto my school dress, everyone will see it when I get off the bus.

I feel my eyes widen and I don't reply. Romy completely gets it just by the look on my face.

'Oh, I'm so hot,' she says really loudly.

She pulls her school jumper off and flicks it onto my lap. I manage a small smile. It makes me think of Jess and the smudge that day, when she didn't have a jumper to tie around her and the rest of us kind of did the job. I tie the jumper around my waist, just in time for our stop.

'Don't worry. I'll get you sorted,' Romy says as we get into the lift. 'You go to the loo and I'll tell Lisa, okay?'

I nod. I hope Dad's not home yet. I'm not sure I want

him to know about this. It's kind of a girl thing. As soon as I think that, my mind swings to Mum. Would she be there for me, like Romy is? Or would she just say something about the tides of life or some other lame, Jason-type thing?

It's Lisa who answers the door, thank god. I just say hi and go straight to the bathroom.

When I check my undies there's less blood than I thought there would be. I realise there would be no chance of it soaking through my dress yet, but there's definitely something there. It's browny and not reddy, just like Jess said. I sit on the loo with my undies halfway down my legs, staring at it.

So, this is it. I have my period. *Hazel Atherton, aged thirteen and four months, has her period.* I look in the mirror and say it aloud, just loud enough for me to hear. It doesn't really sink in. The girl in the mirror stares at me.

'You have your period,' I tell her. 'Finally, you have your period and everything will be different from now on.' She doesn't look that convinced.

There's a knock on the bathroom door.

'Hazel,' says Romy, 'can I come in?'

I take my undies right off and get up to unlock the door. Romy has a fresh pair for me.

'So?' she asks.

I show her.

'Yep, you've got it, girl! Lisa's just gone to the shops to get some pads, because we both only have tampons and you really don't want to use tampons straight away. In the long run I reckon they're better, but –'

Romy stops mid-sentence and gives me a hug. When the hug is over, Romy steps back and she bites her lip and honestly, I think she's about to cry, which is very *un*-Romy.

'Oooh, my baby sister,' she says. 'Well done, you.'

Her voice sounds just like Mum's.

'Knock knock?' Lisa says it rather than does it. The bathroom door is open anyway, but I can see why she hasn't knocked properly. She has a shopping bag in each hand.

'Okay, Hazel, I wasn't sure which ones you'd prefer, so I got them all.'

She's practically carrying the whole selection of sanitary products from the supermarket. Plus, she's got new knickers for me, even though I've got a pair from Romy and a whole stack of them in our bedroom.

'I think this brand is popular,' she says, putting the bags on the bench and opening a packet. 'What do you think, Romy?'

'Let's see,' says Romy, looking through all the packets Lisa has bought, and picking one out. 'These ones are good, Hazel. They have wings, which are the bits that stick out at the side and you can tuck them around undies so the sides are protected.'

Lisa shakes her head. 'They have wings, but they look pretty thin,' she says. 'Maybe these ones are better?' She opens another packet, and then she pauses.

'God, I'm so sorry, Hazel,' she says. 'I haven't even asked you how you're feeling. I guess ... well, I've never done this before. Have you called your mum yet?'

'Yep,' I lie.

Lisa shouldn't feel sorry. She's being great. And Romy is too. They're both trying really hard and paying so much attention to me. I can't remember the last time Mum did. Anyway, I'll call Mum later. She's always on about things happening when you're ready. So, I'll call her when *I'm* ready.

'Okay girls, I'll leave you to it. I'm going to make a special dinner for you, Hazel, now that you're a woman. How about a pumpkin and artichoke pie?'

As soon as Lisa leaves the bathroom, we crack up.

V

Late that night I lie awake. Romy is snoring, but I can't get to sleep. The pad between my legs feels like a nappy. It should be gross, feeling the blood leak onto it, but I'm too relieved to be grossed out. At last it's happened.

I wonder whether people will be able to tell that I'm different. That I've grown up. I'm not sure. I know I'm growing up, but it's like I'm waiting for my emotions to catch up with my body. I guess I do feel different, but not as different as I expected. I still don't know if I'd kiss Leo in the cupboard. It's all pretty confusing.

But there's something else that's even more confusing. My mobile is on my pillow. I could call Mum. She'd still be awake. But each time I pick up my mobile, I put it down again. She'd probably be with Jason and then she'll tell him, and I don't even want Dad to know yet so I definitely don't want Jason to know.

I want my mum. But not the way things are. I want her the way they were.

Eleven

'Dad, can I have the day off?' I ask, when he comes into our room in the morning.

He sits on my bed, leans over and plants a kiss on my forehead. 'You okay?' He pauses for a moment, as if he's considering something. 'Munchkin?' he adds finally.

I realise the something he was considering was whether he can still use his pet name for me, now that I'm not a little girl anymore. Which means Lisa has told him. I'm okay with that. I mean, he is my dad. I just hope he doesn't mention periods or anything. It would be way too weird talking to him about all that. But I'm glad he still calls me munchkin.

'I've still got a bit of a pain,' I say, and I rub my tummy because it's something Dad will understand and I totally don't want to go into details about how the pain is more in my back than my stomach. I don't even get that myself. I guess it's one of the mysteries about periods, but it's not a mystery I want to talk about with Dad. Anyway, I don't feel that bad, but the last few days have been really full-on and I just want a quiet day. Plus, Mum doesn't work on Thursdays. Hopefully, she'll be home by herself for once.

'I'll ring the school,' Dad says. He shakes his head like he's trying to process the knowledge that I'm officially a woman now. 'And congratulations, honey.'

I cringe a little bit, feeling awkward.

I'm still in my PJs and ugg boots when Dad drops me home. Jason's bike is on the porch, again. If I could get back into Dad's car, I would. But he's already driving off.

If I'm really quiet, maybe I'll just be able to sneak into my room and come out when he's gone. I turn my key in the lock and try to be extra quiet as I creep up the hallway.

I'm pretty sure I hear my name mentioned. I creep a little further up the hall and peek around the corner, into the lounge room.

Mum and Jason are talking. About me, I think. I move back a bit and hide, so I can see them but they can't see me. Jason's back is towards me. He has his hand on Mum's shoulder.

Mum sounds like she's been crying, and she keeps telling Jason she's sorry.

He's telling her that it's okay, and that the girls are the most important thing. He's telling her that everything is going to be fine.

He pulls Mum to him and she buries her head in his chest. When she pulls away, her voice is firmer, as though the hug has given her strength.

'… not okay,' she says. '… beautiful daughter … period … not even a phone call.'

Jesus. Dad or Lisa must have called her.

For a second, I feel really annoyed. Mum shouldn't be telling him personal stuff like this. It's my private business. He's the last person in the universe she should be telling.

I'm mad and the feeling rises up through me. Then it whacks into my heart, and collides with another feeling.

Mum should have been the *first* person I told.

She says something I can't make out, then it's Jason talking again.

'You're a beautiful mum, Dee Dee,' Jason says. 'I've seen it … own eyes. Maybe Hazel … in person … phone?'

Mum shakes her head. The next bit is clear.

'Me being with you is driving a wedge between Hazel and me.'

'Dee Dee,' Jason says finally. 'It's okay. I understand.'

He says it like he's resigned to it. Like the relationship is over. Like he's willing to end the relationship. Like they're both willing to end the relationship, actually. For me.

It's horrible. Jason's words, Mum's face. Her tears. I've always hated seeing Mum cry. Then Romy's question pops back into my head. *I think you have to ask yourself whether it's Jason you don't like — or whether you just don't like Mum having a boyfriend.*

Is this really all about Jason, or is it about me not coping with Mum having a boyfriend? I search my mind for what Jason's done wrong. He's messy, he asks too many questions, he uses too much hot water and he puts the butter in the pantry rather than the fridge. But all that stuff seems small. Compared with this.

He kisses my mum and it's a long kiss and I don't want to watch my mum kissing, but I can't help staring. It's pretty wrong, watching my mother hook up. I'm scared that they'll start going further, and, honestly, if they do I think I'll have to cough or something and blow my cover.

Luckily, they pull away from each other.

'I'll get my stuff,' he says quietly.

It was a goodbye kiss.

Mum nods sadly. 'She's having the day off school. She could be home any minute. So maybe that's better.'

I'm worried that he's going to come into the lounge room to get his yoga mat. I need to hurry and it's risky, but I creep over to the mantelpiece and grab the picture of Dad. Then I slip out of the lounge room and down the hall, shutting my bedroom door as quietly as I can.

A few minutes later I hear him close the front door. Then I hear the water running. Mum's in the shower.

I sit on my bed, holding the photo of Dad, me and Romy.

'They've broken up for me,' I tell him. 'They've broken up *because* of me.'

Dad just smiles at me. I put him back on my dresser. It's good to have him back there. It feels right. He shouldn't be in a position to look at Mum's life. He'll always be my dad, but it's none of his business now. He's got his own life, and she has hers.

Maybe I *have* been acting like a little kid. I haven't really been thinking about Jason making Mum happy. I've been thinking about me.

I've got my period now. I'm growing up. That just happened naturally. But maybe it's time *I* change some other things about me too.

I go into Mum's bedroom. She's sitting at her dressing table, brushing her hair. She's beautiful, my mum. It's funny, because I don't usually think of her like that. But she is. She *should* have a boyfriend. If I could choose one for her, it probably wouldn't be Jason. But it's her choice.

'Hazel!' she says when she sees me. 'You must've come

in while I was in the shower.' She gets up and walks over to me. 'So, it's happened. That's great, honey. I'm so pleased for you.'

Mum wraps her arms around me. We haven't hugged for ages. At first, it feels stiff, but she doesn't let me go. And I don't want her to let me go. When she finally does release me, she still has hold of my shoulders.

'My baby,' she says softly. 'My *grown-up* baby.'

She's smiling with her mouth but not with her eyes. She's trying too hard to be bright and happy.

'So, where were you when it started?' she asks, pulling me over to sit on her bed. It's unmade and I know that Jason slept in it last night while Romy and I were at Dad and Lisa's. Yesterday, that would have rankled me.

'I was on the bus,' I say. 'Not the most exotic location.'

Mum laughs. Her eyes join in this time.

'How are you feeling?' she asks. 'Any pain? I could make you a hot water bottle. It can help if you have a sore stomach. I always carry the pain in my back.'

I'm like Mum. Carrying the pain in my back. It's strange, but that makes me feel more … normal, I guess.

'That's where I've been sore too,' I say. Then I shake my head. 'I don't need a hot water bottle, thanks. I feel okay. I needed a day off, though.'

'Well, it's a big thing, Hazel. It's fine for you to have a day off. You need some time to let it sink in that you've crossed a threshold.' She laughs a short laugh. 'Actually, I'm glad it's my day off too. So *I* can let it sink in that my baby has become a woman.'

'Do I look any different?' I ask. I know it's a stupid question, but I'm glad I'm here with my mum and it's okay to ask stupid questions. Mum leans back and looks at me.

'Hmmm,' she says, 'there *is* something different, I reckon. Maybe it's the look in your eyes. A bit more depth or wisdom perhaps?'

It sounds like something Jason might say. I like it, actually, but I'm not sure whether it's true.

I take a deep breath. 'Mum, I heard you and Jason when you were in the kitchen.'

Mum looks thoughtful as she takes that in. 'Oh well, Hazel,' she says. 'I'll be fine. Maybe it's not the right time for me and Jason. It will be just the three of us again. The three musketeers, eh?' She says it bravely, as though the choice was hers and had nothing to do with me.

But I heard what they were saying. I heard how upset she really was. She's just trying to protect me.

I have that familiar pang of missing Mum so much. Weird, when she's sitting right beside me. I guess it's more that I *have* missed her so much.

'Mum, I don't think ...' I begin. But I don't know exactly how to say this. 'It's just ...'

'Hazel,' Mum says, looking at me with a small smile, 'use your words.' It's an old joke between us. When I was little and throwing a tantrum, Mum used to say that. It makes me smile to hear it again, but it also makes me want to find the right words.

'Mum, I don't want you to break up with Jason,' I say. 'He's all right. At least he can cook.'

Mum looks confused. 'But I thought ...' She trails off, and it's Mum who can't find the right words now.

'It's just that so much has changed around here since you met him,' I say. 'Maybe ... maybe we can just make some rules about him?'

'Rules?' Mum asks.

'Yeah, like the butter goes in the fridge, not the pantry. That sort of thing.'

Mum shakes her head, but she's smiling. 'Okay,' she says slowly. 'What else?'

'Four-minute showers, so he doesn't waste the hot water.'

'And?'

'We keep our Thursday nights. Just us.'

'Pizzas and chick flicks?'

'Yep, no boys allowed.'

Mum takes my face in her hands, squeezing my cheeks together. 'And you'd be okay with him – you'd be okay with Jason in our lives – if we follow those rules?'

I don't know if it's getting my period or I'm getting more grown-up or whatever it is, but it's like things are starting fresh and I've found my *words* and I like it.

'I would,' I say with a grin. 'But just one more thing. Get him to cut off his dreadlocks.'

Mum's laugh is loud and true. 'Don't push it, Hazel.'

'Are you watching the movie or are you on the computer?' Mum says.

The three of us are in our PJs. I've been in mine all day. Mum and I are sharing the couch and Romy is lying on the carpet.

'Both,' I say.

Mum rolls her eyes, but I can tell she's happy. Her mobile rings and now it's my turn to roll my eyes. It's obvious from her face that it's Jason. She left him a message and he's calling her back.

'Are you watching the movie or are you on the phone?' I tease.

Romy pauses the DVD and we make kissy faces at Mum as she answers the call. She takes it into the kitchen and I look back at the computer screen.

Edi's on Facebook and she's left a message for me.

Where were u today, slackarse? Wagging? Went down to the tree at recess and guess wot? Leo asked where u were! Everyone reckons he's going to ask u out! So u better be at school tomoz!!! Wot u going 2 say?

I can't believe it. It might not even be true. It might just be a rumour. But how seriously weird would it be if Leo asked me out the day after I got my period? Honestly, it would be like one of Jason's theories about everything being linked and the Earth's energy and stuff.

I decide not to write anything about Leo just yet.

Can't wait 'til the caravan meeting tomoz! I type.

It's so cool that's all I need to write. I know Edi will get it. She does.

OMG Hazel. Finally! Hooorrraaay! Caravan meeting asap! Will check with the others. Go you!

I can't stop smiling. I wonder if anyone at school will be able to tell what's happened?

For a moment, I think Edi must have gone off to do something, but then some more words appear onscreen.

Can u believe Archie hasn't even asked me yet?? And Leo's going 2 ask you tomoz? He's so nice … u shld say yes. But wot will I do about Archie?

This is pretty much the first time in history Edi has asked for my advice.

Just hang in there, Edi. He likes u 4 sure! Gtg x

I know it will drive her crazy that I haven't told her what I'll say to Leo if he asks me out. It would be pretty wild if that happened before Archie got around to asking Edi. I totally thought it would happen to her first.

Part of me thinks I'd say yes. The other part is a bit too freaked out by what it might mean to have a boyfriend. Especially an older boyfriend. Will he just want to kiss, or would he want to do more than that?

Mum comes back into the lounge.

'Well?' says Romy, taking a bite of cold pizza. 'What did he say?'

'Don't speak with your mouth full, Romy,' Mum says. 'It's disgusting.'

'Wha id he thay?' Romy repeats, and it's even more gross this time cos I can see the half-chewed pizza in her mouth.

Mum shakes her head. 'He says that we're a very weird family and that butter really *should* go in the pantry,' she says with a smile. 'And he said he'll do it anyway.'

Mum's beaming and I feel good. I helped her to feel this way. Or at least I've stopped making her miserable.

'Actually,' I find myself saying. 'Someone likes me too. I think.'

'Who?' Romy and Mum ask at the same time.

'Leo,' I say. 'He's in the year above me.'

'Ooh, I don't know about that,' Mum says. 'If you're going to date, then shouldn't it be someone your own age?'

'Mum, Dad was *five* years older than you,' Romy points out. 'And you *married* him.'

'Hmmm,' Mum says. 'Well, I guess it all depends on what kind of boy he is.'

I think of how Leo calmed Nick down that day. I think

of how cute he was at Archie's party, before the whole truth or dare thing.

'He's really nice,' I say.

'Good,' Romy says. 'Can we watch the movie now?' She presses play on the remote.

I shift around on the couch. As I do, the pad in my undies feels heavy.

'Romy,' I say, 'can you pause it? I think I need to go to the bathroom.'

Romy throws her arms up in the air. 'You guys are *hopeless*,' she says, but she does press the pause button again. 'I brought back a packet of tampons Lisa bought. They're on the bench and there's a leaflet inside the box to show you how to use them if you want to have a go. They're way better than pads. You can barely feel them.'

'Romy!' Mum says. 'Hazel's had her period for less than twenty-four hours. Don't rush her.'

'Maybe next time, Romy,' I say, and as I say it I get a woozy feeling. As though it's sinking in. This is going to happen again and again. My body has changed forever. If I had sex, which I totally won't, I could have a baby!

It's a big change. But the weirdest change is right here in the lounge room. It's my mum and my sister. Like it used to be, but with adjustments, and it feels fine. Actually it feels better than fine.

I go to the bathroom and then wander into the kitchen to get a drink.

'Gonna be long?' Romy calls out.

I don't answer. I want to spend time with my new self, and I know I won't be able to focus on the movie anyway.

This is the all-new Hazel Atherton getting juice out of the fridge, I tell myself. *This is the all-new Hazel Atherton pouring juice into a glass.*

'Hazel!' Romy yells.

This is the all-new Hazel Atherton being yelled at by Romy.

When I close the fridge door, I see the appointment card for my doctor's visit. I don't need to go now. In a way, Mum was right. My body did its own thing in its own time.

I take the card off the fridge and throw it in the bin.

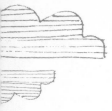

GIRL V THE WORLD

I Heart You, Archie de Souza

Edi lives a weird double life. At school it seems like everyone loves her, but at home her parents barely notice she exists – except when her marks aren't good enough.

So when Edi hooks up with her crush Archie, she can hardly believe her luck. Archie is super cute, and his family are warm and welcoming. Edi wants to spend every waking minute with Archie, even if it means letting her friends and schoolwork slide. But does Archie feel the same way?

Things I Don't Know

Leni doesn't understand her friends or family *at all*. Why does Anya want to start a dumb kissing competition? Why won't her grandmother quit smoking? And why is her athletics buddy Adam acting like a big weirdo around her?

The Leni meets Jo ... the new girl at school. She's cool and fun, and totally on Leni's wavelength. But as their friendship grows, Leni finds she has questions about Jo too. Or maybe they are questions about herself. Whatever it is, she doesn't know the answers!

It's Not Me, It's You

Erin doesn't know exactly *when* it happened, but it happened. Boys started being boyfriends. Girls started wearing make-up to school. And her big sister started keeping secrets about her love-life.

It seems like everyone is changing around Erin, and yet she's still the same. She's fine doing her own thing, but she never thought she'd be deliberately left out. How can Erin grow up *and* just be herself?

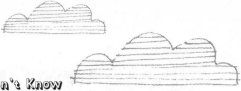